ROOT BOUND

BOOK 5

THE ELEMENTAL SERIES

PRAISE FOR THE ELEMENTAL SERIES

"I love Shannon's Rylee Adamson series . . . and I was wonderfully surprised that I loved her Elemental Series even more!"

-Denise Grover Swank
USAT & NYT Bestselling Author of the "Chosen Series"

"I could not put it down and greedily consumed it in one sitting!"

-Books In Veins

"I think Larkspur aka Lark is the new heroine to watch out for . . ."

-Coffee Book Mom Reviews

"What a fantastic start to a new fantasy series! I love a strong female lead and we were delivered that in spades with Larkspur . . . This story is fast paced and exciting right from the start. I can't wait to see what comes next!"

-Boundless Book Reviews

ROOT BOUND

BOOK 5

THE ELEMENTAL SERIES

SHANNON MAYER

USA TODAY BESTSELLING AUTHOR OF *RECURVE*

ALSO BY SHANNON MAYER

THE RYLEE ADAMSON NOVELS

Priceless (Book 1)
Immune (Book 2)
Raising Innocence (Book 3)
Shadowed Threads (Book 4)
Blind Salvage (Book 5)
Tracker (Book 6)
Veiled Threat (Book 7)
Wounded (Book 8)
Rising Darkness (Book 9)
Blood of the Lost (Book 10)
Alex (A Short Story)
Tracking Magic (A Novella 0.25)
Elementally Priceless (A Novella 0.5)
Guardian (A Novella 6.5)
Stitched (A Novella 8.5)

THE RYLEE ADAMSON EPILOGUES

RYLEE (Book 1)
LIAM (Book 2)

THE ELEMENTAL SERIES

Recurve (Book 1)
Breakwater (Book 2)
Firestorm (Book 3)
Windburn (Book 4)
Rootbound (Book 5)

THE BLOOD BORNE SERIES

(Written with Denise Grover Swank)
Recombinant (Book 1)
Replica (Book 2)

THE NEVERMORE TRILOGY

The Nevermore Trilogy
Sundered (Book 1)
Bound (Book 2)
Dauntless (Book 3)

A CELTIC LEGACY

A Celtic Legacy
Dark Waters (Book 1)
Dark Isle (Book 2)
Dark Fae (Book 3)

THE RISK SERIES

(Written as S.J. Mayer)
High Risk Love (Book 1)

CONTEMPORARY ROMANCES

(Written as S.J. Mayer)
Of The Heart

SETTING

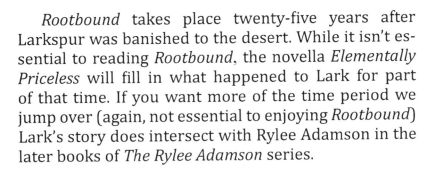

Rootbound takes place twenty-five years after Larkspur was banished to the desert. While it isn't essential to reading *Rootbound*, the novella *Elementally Priceless* will fill in what happened to Lark for part of that time. If you want more of the time period we jump over (again, not essential to enjoying *Rootbound*) Lark's story does intersect with Rylee Adamson in the later books of *The Rylee Adamson* series.

ROOTBOUND

*When a potted plant has outgrown its container, the roots become entangled and matted together, and the growth of the plant becomes **stunted**. When repotting, loosen and **tear** the roots on the edges of the root ball, **forcing** them to once again grow outward.*

CHAPTER 1

"You know, I don't mind following you, Lark, because the view is truly enjoyable with the sway of your hips, the sweet lines of your body and the way your hair swirls on the air, but maybe you could at least talk to me? It's been months. *Months* and not a word," Cactus said between gasps. "Do I not deserve at least a word? Something?"

I slowed my pace, my mind so caught up in what we'd survived when many had fallen that I didn't realize how long it had been. I'd eaten, slept, walked and run, then done it all again. The freedom to move had pulsed through me.

I looked around us, and knew that the wandering was coming to an end. We'd nearly reached the Rim, our home in the Redwoods. The power of the earth coursed through all three sets of our veins as we'd traveled. Peta was at my side in her snow leopard form. She loped along with an easy stride, her ears flicking to me as Cactus spoke. The bond between us vibrated with irritation. She understood my silence and had embraced it with me.

Cactus was right, I hadn't spoken to him, yet that decision had nothing to do with him, and everything to do with what we'd recently lived through. What my mind was dealing with.

In a matter of a week, I'd been released from my second punishment in an oubliette. Rylee, the Tracker, had freed me from the prison I could not escape on my own. I'd rallied the four elemental families to help fight the demon hordes, and battled said horde side by side with Rylee, her family, and the supernaturals left in the world.

Twenty-five years ago, I'd been banished to the desert for helping a Tracker. My father had only seen what I'd done as breaking the rules, not realizing that there was more to stepping outside the parameters of being an elemental. While in the desert, I'd met a second Tracker, and helped her as well. Once more my father punished me, only seeing the letter of the law, and not the spirit. He couldn't see that in breaking the rules, I'd done my best to help save lives. Regardless, Father had seen fit to punish me yet again and had sentenced me once more into an oubliette.

Another six years of my life had passed in that darkness, my mind fighting to stay sane in my second spell within an oubliette. I was freed by Rylee as she fought to save the world from a demon horde. Which meant as soon as I was released, I was thrust into a battle for the world, my friends and family at my side. The battle was one we'd barely survived, and a good many of those I'd known and loved hadn't.

To say I was struggling with the company of others was a small understatement.

A scene of the battle crashed over me, as suffocating as an ocean of water holding me below the waves, forcing itself down my throat.

Demons swarmed. Their weapons swept in terrifying arcs

toward those at my side. The world was dark with droves of them. One fell, and ten took its place. Supernaturals, elementals, and friends died faster than we could kill the demons.

I'd grasped the Tracker's spirit in my hands while her heart beat its final thump and then watched as, with a Daywalker shaman's help, we brought her back to life, making her something new and more dangerous than she'd been before, if that was possible. It was the only way to save her. A part of me knew she would hate me for it, and I accepted that burden.

We had stopped the demons, but lost so much in the process.

The demons were sucked back into their realm deep within the Veil, finally locked away.

And that was when the elementals began to fight one another like the fools they were. What had driven them to that? My sister, the queen of the Rim, tried to stop them. Tried to be the peacemaker and bring them to see reason. It hadn't worked.

A shiver rolled through me as I tried to blink the vision away. The fear of screwing up once more and the world paying for my failure nipped at me. An old fear, and one I thought I'd given up while I'd rotted in the oubliette.

What the world had barely escaped, without even realizing, was so heavy on my mind that words couldn't encompass the last few months. Between that and truly believing I was free of my prison, the words would not come, and all I'd been able to do was move and give silence. An homage to what was almost my fate if I'd fallen on the battle field. Silence in death was a lot longer than a twenty-year banishment, or even my years in the oubliette.

But that was Cactus for you; he never really felt the depth of the world around us or the weight of responsibility that lay on our shoulders as elementals. After twenty-five plus years of his own banishment, he hadn't learned a thing. I'd hoped he would gain some insight during his own time away from the world, that he'd grow up at least a little and see outside his own needs and desires.

I shared a glance with Peta. Her ashen coat blended into the clouds around us. The thick tumultuous gray blanket rumbled, again, drawing my attention and making me twitch. Peta's green eyes rolled skyward.

"Lark. Talk to me. Please." Cactus's voice broke. "I . . . did I do something wrong? I feel like I'm missing something. Like you're angry with me. I can't bear it."

I slowed to a stop and looked back at him. His eyes were close to the same shade of green as Peta's: vibrant and full of life and laughter. His dark red hair was mussed from the speed at which we'd traveled, the wind having whipped it into a maelstrom of strands that mimicked a live flame and half his elemental heritage.

I stared hard at him, knowing in that moment in my heart and soul, he was not the one for me. I'd felt that certainty grow over the months of silence. No matter how much I loved him, no matter how much history we shared, we would soon part ways for the final time. I felt it in every bone and fiber of my body. And maybe that was partly why I'd postponed going home, to delay the inevitable.

In that, Peta was right. Cactus would never be able to stand with me in the things I had to face, or the path I had to walk. A tiny piece of my heart broke and I let it go, breathing through the pain and tightness in my chest. My first friend.

My first real love.

But he was . . . not right, not for me. And that truth, ah, it stung as deeply as any wound I'd ever had, perhaps deeper. The part of me that was still the little girl who'd loved him so fiercely didn't want to let him go.

But the woman I'd become knew better.

"Talk to me, Lark." He whispered my name as he stepped close, and his hands closed on mine, the closest I'd let him get to me since the battle. The heat of his skin warmed my fingers, stealing my resistance to his charm. I made myself pull away. "Let me help you, please. I gave you room when you needed it, followed you all over this continent without questioning why you ran without thought."

We stared at each other. How could he not understand my silence? How could he be so blind to what had happened? He'd been there at the battle; surely he'd seen the price we paid to defeat Orion and his demon army. Did he feel nothing for those we'd lost, for the things we'd seen and done to save the world?

His eyes were full of sorrow, but not for anyone else. The worry was for his own desires, his own needs. I took a breath and broke my silence, my voice hitching on some of the words from lack of use.

"There were more deaths in the elemental world and the supernatural world . . . facing Orion and his demon horde . . . than we have ever seen. Their deaths mean that you and I and Peta have survived. Can I not honor them the way I see fit? To acknowledge that without them, my silence would be eternal?"

His eyes dropped along with his shoulders. He ran a hand over his head and scrubbed at his hair, messing it further. "I'm a selfish ass."

"Yes, *that* is true. Nice that you can finally acknowledge it." I turned and walked away, but not before his head snapped up, his eyes flashing with irritation.

Peta sneezed, shifted, and leapt for my arms. I caught her and she placed herself on my shoulder, balancing easily as I strode forward. "Apparently that wasn't the response he hoped for."

Apparently. I nodded, but reined in my words. Silence for the dead . . . I didn't say what I had only to shut Cactus up. Those who had fought at our sides and fallen, their deaths were all around me. The faces of those we'd known and depended on, friends, allies, and brilliant fighters. Dead. Lost to the other side of the Veil.

Gone.

Ashes to ashes.

Ash. His name tightened around me like a serpent coiling its body, constricting every breath I took until I was forced to slow my feet. That was the other reason I'd run. I'd thought he'd find me. I thought Ash would seek me out but he hadn't. I'd seen nothing of him as I'd silently crossed the continent and the fear in me had grown. Ash would never have left me. Peta dug her thin claws into my shirt until their tips brushed my shoulder. "What is it? There is a pain in you I have felt only when we are separated. A loss so deep, it can only be of someone your heart rightly belongs to. But your family survived the battle. What is it?"

A rumble across the sky drew my attention and whatever I might have said stalled in my throat.

Clouds formed in deep-gray tumbling masses that rolled over one another toward us. Distracted, I didn't answer her right away. Or maybe I wasn't ready to say his name out loud.

"Yes, Bella and the others survived. But . . ." I kept my eyes glued to the sky, looking for even the slightest twitch of lightning deliberately not answering the first part of her question.

I didn't have to.

"You mean Ash, don't you?" she said softly. It hadn't gotten past either of us that he was "put away" somewhere while still under my father's rule. Not an oubliette, but closer to a banishment. From what Peta told me, he snuck back to the edge of the Rim every few months to soak in our home and recharge. Without doing that, he'd have gone insane in a few short years.

My conversation after the battle with Blossom, a fellow Ender from the Rim, had left me shaken.

Ash had not come back for over a year; even though my sister Bella, the new queen of the Rim, lifted the banishment on him, he'd not returned.

Cactus drew up beside me, his eyes going skyward.

"You think we have trouble?"

Peta snorted. "Please, Lark is nothing but trouble. There is only one person who outstrips her in that, and she's no longer an issue."

Rylee. Tracker and savior of the world was an even bigger magnet than me when it came to chaos and strife. Seeing as we had common blood in the power of Spirit, it shouldn't have been a surprise. But Peta was right: Rylee was no longer an issue, seeing as how we'd stripped her of the very thing that made her that magnet. Which meant I was now number one in the world when it came to trouble making.

Go me.

"Lark, we will be at the Rim soon. We will be able to rest, eat, heal. And we can talk about this, about what we're going to do now that you don't have to save the world. You can have a life now, a family if you want, a home you aren't always trying to protect." Cactus grinned as he rubbed a hand up and down his own arm several times.

Still I couldn't seem to find the words to speak to him.

At least not the words he wanted from me. I strode ahead, knowing that until I made it clear we were done as anything but friends, he would follow me.

"He will get over you. But you have to let him go. You

have to make him see you will not change your mind." Peta pressed the side of her face against my cheek, rubbing gently.

She was right, and it was time I cut him loose. Told him to go his own way, find his own life and his own love, and forget about me and any foolish dreams he had of making a relationship work between us.

There would be no home for me, not like he meant. I would return to the Rim, always. But my feet no longer needed the feel of the forest under them. Not the way the other Terralings did. With Spirit running through my veins, the world was open to me. I was not bound to one place as the other elementals were.

I drew in the breath to say the words that would send Cactus away. Hard words that made me pause as they rested on the tip of my tongue.

A crack of lightning over our heads lit up the air with electricity, and the treetops seemed to shudder in fear. My hair rose, floating on the breeze around my face, and I immediately tapped into the earth, grounding me solidly.

Power flooded me, pushing away thoughts of Cactus. I sank my feet into the soil, and held myself steady. There was no way some errant Sylph was going to rip me from the ground and bat me around like a kitty toy.

Another crack of lightning followed by a boom of thunder kept me where I was, hanging onto the earth, prepping myself for a fight. But no Sylph appeared.

"Perhaps we should take shelter," Cactus said over the rising wind. He had no idea I'd even tapped into the earth. That was a gift only I had: the ability to see when other elementals were about to use their power.

Slowly I let go of the power beneath my feet. It probably said something that I immediately thought the storm was elemental-made, and designed to kick my ass, when in fact, it was nothing more than a bad storm.

Clouds rolled as though they boiled, and the lightning picked up speed along with the thunder. Each boom shook my body, echoing inside my chest like a mighty drum. The smell of ozone filled the air, teasing my nose with its acrid scent.

Cactus trotted ahead of me, straight for a driveway that wound through the trees, stopping when he waved at a human's cabin sitting on the edge of a ravine, facing west, the direction the storm rolled from.

I say cabin, but the place was closer to a mansion. Two stories, the entire front of the house was windows and a large deck wrapped around the whole thing. I followed, slowly, while the wind whipped around me, tugging at my clothes and limbs. The gale came sharply, the wind smacked and pulled me sideways.

The windows of the house blinked like oversized eyes as they caught the shadows and light of the clouds rolling by, malignant and evil, the deck like a strange wooden mouth waiting to snare me when I stepped onto it.

The past haunts you. You know that. The voice was my own, no other. But of a saner me, a kinder me. The girl I'd left behind when I'd stepped out of the oubliette the first time. A girl I wasn't sure even existed, it had been so long since I'd heard her voice. Certainly not after my second round in the oubliette. Punishment for helping Rylee save a child from a shadow walker. I shook my head. The world was far from fair. I knew that.

But just once, I'd like it to swing in my favor.

Peta leapt from my shoulder and shifted into her snow leopard form. Hurrying ahead of me, she was on the steps of the porch before she paused and looked back.

"Lark."

"I'm not going in there." I angled toward the space under the large deck. Cactus laughed and I ignored him. The very thought of stuffing myself into a man-made house sent my heart rate skyrocketing like a hummingbird's.

The space between the bottom of the deck and earth was about three feet high. Big enough for me to slip in and find a pillar of wood to put my back against. I ducked under, wiping away the cobwebs that brushed across my face, and the smell of small animals that had used the space as a shelter. I settled down, sinking my feet and ass into the loose dirt as an anchor in case the wind managed to tug on me.

Peta crept in with me, her eyes worried, but she said nothing, only lay at my side and put her head onto my lap. A soft purr rumbled through her. I placed my hand on her back, her presence soothing me.

"I missed you so very much, my friend," I whispered.

She flipped a big paw over my thigh. "Never again, Lark. Where you go, I go, no matter the consequences. I cannot live with my heart missing from me. I will not do it again."

I closed my eyes, leaned forward, and pressed my face into the back of her neck. "Let it be so."

A tiny trill of agreement tripped out of her. I sat up, opened my eyes, and fought not to grab my spear.

Cactus peered over the lip of the deck, hanging upside down, smiling. But the smile looked like a frown, a death mask with his white teeth grinning and his hair stuck up all over. I sucked in a sharp breath as he reached out for me.

"Come inside, Lark. There are beds and the walls keep the wind out."

Beds. Did he think I was going to fall into his arms and strip off my clothes? Idiot.

"No."

"You're just being stubborn again. You don't need to. I know you're tough. I know you are strong and beautiful. You don't need to prove anything to me." He dropped over the edge, flipping in the air so he landed in a crouch. He rubbed his hands into the soil, and a trickle of green ran down his arms.

"Making me flowers isn't going to change my mind," I said.

He startled. "How did you know?"

I shrugged. "A gift."

He smiled. "So not a surprise, but you deserve it anyway." A multitude of flowers erupted from the soil on long stalks, blooming around me in a matter of seconds. In under a minute the tiny space was full of every spring flower, every color, every scent from lavender to rose. Some I'd seen and some I'd not, some I had no idea what they were, which was impressive.

For a moment, it felt as though we were back in the Rim, hiding from our parents. Unaware of the world and the danger it held for us. For a moment, I could believe I was that little girl again, and he was going to be my prince.

The moment passed like the sun setting in one last burst of light before the darkness claims the sky; one last moment of defiance before it was done.

He crept in and sat on the other side of me. "I know I can be an ass."

I closed my eyes. The last thing I wanted was an apology. "Don't say anything more, Cactus—"

"I want to have that conversation now. The one you've been putting off. For years, if we are being honest." He took my hand, and pressed it between his. "Lark. I love you, and nothing you say or do will change that. We love each other . . . I've loved you since we were children. That has to count for something."

With my eyes closed and the smell of the earth and flowers infusing my skin and senses, it would have been easy to give in. But the raging storm and the sound of the trees creaking as they swayed were as strong in my ears as the scent of the flowers in my nose and on my tongue. There would never be peace in my life, not the way Cactus wanted. He didn't understand.

Ash did. Ash knew me and knew I would always have to fight, that there would be no peace for me. Which was why I had to find him. He understood me in ways Cactus could never.

"I cannot be that person in your life, Cactus. I . . . don't love you the way you want. Or deserve."

"Bullshit." His voice was soft as he leaned forward, his lips at the edge of my face.

Peta didn't move, but a long low growl slipped out of her. "Prick, you push too far. Just like you always do because you are a selfish shit. She tells you the truth and you ignore her. Demand that she change her mind. Try to ply her with the emotions she *does* have for you. That is not love. That is manipulation and an attempt to control her."

Her words resonated in my heart, and I opened my eyes, narrowing them as I did. Cactus was right in front of me, his face a breath from mine. I put a hand on his chest and pushed. "Back up."

The hurt in his eyes was instant. "It's not like that. I'm not trying to make you do anything. I think you get confused because of all the things that have happened and I just want you to see—"

Anger snapped along my spine as if the lightning outside our cover had struck my body. "I . . . get confused?"

Peta drew back and from the corner of my eye she shook her head. "Stupid. Very stupid, Prick."

"Not like that. I mean . . ." He drew a breath. "This is two against one, you know. This conversation is between you and me. Not you, me, and your pussy cat."

I pressed my hand into the earth in front of me and drew the power away from the plants he'd created until every last one shriveled into dried-up husks, the smell of the spring blooms dying on the air. I could have let go, but I didn't. I kept drawing on the power of the earth, pulling all it would give me. Peta let out a squeak and Cactus shifted back until he was at the edge of the opening.

"I think it's time you left." The power roaring through me made my words hum and reverberate in the air.

"You've changed," he said. "You aren't the girl I fell in love with. That I've loved all these years. You aren't yourself anymore, Lark."

And then he was gone, back up to the human house to hide from me.

What had he said? That he would love me no matter what? So he'd either been lying or he was doing exactly as Peta said.

Making an attempt to manipulate me with the last of the love he knew lay between us.

The rage that lit me up was like nothing I'd ever felt.

Not even when I'd seen the truth of Bella's past, and the abuse she suffered at the hands of Cassava, her mother. Watching my sister being beaten and manipulated as a child, through her own memories had been the fist time I'd truly unleashed my strength. The first time anger took my power and cast it far and wide in an arc of destruction. Since then, I'd been careful, so very careful not to lose control.

This moment eclipsed that anger. Not when I'd discovered the mother goddess was leading me by the nose to remove the rulers of the other families and replace them with the rulers of her choice had I been so hurt. Not even when I'd faced Blackbird and realized he was stronger than me, that I was at his mercy, had I been so frustrated.

I stumbled out from under the deck and ran to the edge of the cliff where the soft dirt met solid rock. Gathering the strength of the earth deep in my soul, I let it out, driven by rage, powered by pain and humiliation, and under it all, strengthened by Spirit.

I had no idea what I was doing, but for once, I didn't care.

Spirit all but sang as I tapped into it, weaving it around the power of the earth until the two elements were a blur of colors racing up and down my arms, a beautiful twinning of deep green and the softest of pinks.

"What does he think? That I could survive two oubliettes and remain unchanged?" I screamed into the raging wind. "That I could survive the last battle that nearly ended our world and remain the weak maiden he knew as a child?"

The words were stripped from my lips as I said them, but they weren't for anyone but myself. "That I would be the one he could tuck away from the world? That I would be his subservient wife? That I would let *him* be my hero?"

Peta was at my side, her paws wrapped around my lower leg, hanging onto me with all she had. She might have spoken, but I couldn't hear it over my screams and the increasing storm. Couldn't hear her over the emotions ripping through me as surely as the storm that kissed the land.

"I am my own hero. *I* will slay the dragons. I need no one to save me."

The world heaved under me, Peta cried out . . . and I lost control of my power.

CHAPTER 2

y power took on a life of its own as it ramped up, increasing in leaps and bounds. I closed my eyes and mentally reached for both Spirit and Earth, doing all I could to draw them to me, to calm the raging powers. Like grabbing at wet reins on a runaway horse, the hold I had was tenuous, at best.

Sweat poured from me as I struggled, fighting to pull it together.

Spirit was completely out of control, writhing around me, almost as if it were an entity all its own. And it wanted the power of the earth to rise and destroy things, to break free of my hold on it, to shatter the land.

Worm shit and green sticks, goblin shit and goose guts. This was not what I'd been planning. Not that I'd thought much about what I was doing. I'd been so filled with rage, I couldn't hold back. I needed to let it out.

The sweat droplets rolled down my body in tiny rivers. As the sky opened up, rain joined the sweat, soaking me through as the edge of the ravine trembled under me. The rain chilled my skin, and sent steam curling from me. I gritted my teeth and with my eyes still closed, I focused everything I had on bringing my powers to heel.

The sound of rocks falling, the crack of stone, the steady trickle of pebbles sliding over the edge were all I heard. The earth beneath us groaned and tipped, as if it would buck me off into the abyss.

What the hell was happening? Why couldn't I control my elements?

If I didn't do something soon, both Peta and I would fall to our deaths.

The thought of Peta dying spurred my efforts. I took a stranglehold of Spirit and drew it to me, calming it, whispering that I would learn, pushing it back. Earth was easier once I had Spirit under control.

I opened my eyes, and realized I'd fallen to my knees at some point. I slung an arm over Peta's shoulders. "That was too close."

She shuddered. "I thought you had more time, but it looks as though you are closer to the edge than I thought." Her green eyes blinked up at me and she pointed with a paw at the ravine. "No pun intended."

"What do you mean . . . you thought I had more time?" I panted for breath around the words.

"Spirit needs to be trained. That is what I learned in my studies. Until it does, it will do this to you: steal your control and make you fight to do what you wish."

I frowned and wobbled to my feet. The rage had burned out with the power and fear, a combination that left me exhausted beyond what I thought possible. "Are you sure?"

She nodded. "Yes. You had no control. I felt it through the bond. Spirit is gaining strength and until you understand it, it will make your life . . . difficult. Not impossible, just harder."

"And if there is no training?" Because who the hell would I ask to show me the ropes? Cassava? I think not.

"You will burn out your powers, leaving you an empty husk."

"Oh, well if that's all." I drew a breath and brushed a hand over my face, wiping off rain and sweat.

"Do not take this lightly," she chastised.

I held a hand out to her. "I'm not. I just . . . I'm exhausted."

Cactus stumbled up to us, his brows drawn in two deep slashes. He raised his voice to be heard over the howl of the wind. "Why did you do that? You could have killed someone."

His unsaid words were that I could have killed him too.

"But I didn't kill anyone. Did I?" I put a hand on my spear, balancing myself against a particularly hard gust of wind, the rain slapping at us—at this elevation, more ice than rain. Around us branches snapped in half and were flung with a violence that seemed as if the trees were attempting to spear us. Several landed at my feet, plunged into the ground like fallen arrows. From above, a squirrel chattered incessantly as if that would somehow slow the pace of the frenzied storm whipping around us. Or maybe he was thinking the same thing as me. That Cactus talked when he had no idea of what he spoke.

"Didn't think about humans, did you?" Cactus stood and scanned the horizon, the accusation clear in his voice.

I narrowed my eyes. "Nothing happened, Cactus. And even if I had dropped off that edge, anyone foolish enough to risk being in a storm of this size deserves what they get. In particular the humans." Anger coursed through me again, lighting a flame I thought I'd banked by throwing my weight around.

His eyes flicked to me and then away. "You won't scare me from you, Lark."

I threw my hands in the air, fully and totally exasperated. Making my way to the deck, I ducked under and sat against what I thought of as my pillar. Peta didn't ease off the side of my leg as I crept through the short space.

Cactus ducked down, and I pointed a finger at him. "No. Go up to the house. I don't want you in here."

His jaw ticked and he spun on his heel, a flick of pebbles spraying out behind him, he moved so fast.

His feet on the deck pounded a steady thud that was gone swiftly. I leaned forward and wrapped my arms around Peta, burying my face in her thick fur as a sigh escaped me. The warmth of her body and the steady rumble of her purr soothed me enough that I rested.

The storm raged, lashing the deck until it creaked and the wood sounded as though it held on by mere splinters. None of that mattered as fatigue rolled over me, pulling me under its spell completely. For the first time in days, I let myself sleep, falling into a place I feared like no other, and only because I clung to my familiar.

"I am here, Lark. I will not leave you," she whispered into my ear as she curled around me, sharing with me not only her warmth but her strength too.

My dreams were fitful and full of death, blood, violence and an urgency I couldn't place. The world was safe. The demons defeated. Yet the sense of time slipping through my fingers remained.

The feeling that I was missing something integral, something I needed to understand, yet couldn't see was overwhelming.

What could possibly be driving the emotions that fired my adrenaline and jerked me awake, sweating and panting for breath? The darkness disoriented me and for a terrifying soul-sucking moment, I was entombed, held by man-made material I couldn't escape, once more in an oubliette.

I lurched forward, stumbling over Peta's sleeping form. She let out a cry, but I barely acknowledged her, barely recalled she was with me, so turned around as I was in my mind. Believing I was once again confined, swallowed by a prison I couldn't fight.

Scrambling on my hands and knees, I spilled out from under the deck and onto the hard-packed dirt. Fear nipped at me, and I drove my hands into the loose earth, letting the power slowly fill my soul, and drive the haunting ghosts back. No one could take me while I held the earth's power.

Except Blackbird. A shudder rippled down my spine. Blackbird . . . Raven . . . one and the same. My younger brother had betrayed our family, destroying so much of the Rim, I wasn't sure it would ever come back.

A soft wind blew through the trees, and the sharp tang of pitch and decaying earth filled my lungs. I drew it in and out, slow and even as I calmed my racing heart. This was the smell of home. The fresh scent coaxed the fear out of me piece by piece. The moon hung heavy over the treetops, its light reflecting off the tips, tinting them silver in the darkness. In the aftermath of the storm, the world was peaceful, clean, and safe once more.

Peta trotted to my side. "I hear Cactus snoring. We could leave him and be home in a matter of hours."

I grinned at her, though my lips wobbled. "I knew there was a reason I kept you around."

She snorted and I took a step away from the cabin. I paused and looked back, the wide black windows staring at me still. How he could sleep in there, I had no idea. I shuddered and hurried away.

The trees and darkness away from the cabin didn't bother me, not a bit.

"Tell me again what you know of Ash's disappearance." I pushed a low-hanging branch out of my way.

"Nothing more than what we both know. He hasn't been back for a year, despite Bella lifting the banishment—"

"That has only been a few weeks. Not long enough for him to hear about it," I said.

"But Griffin couldn't find him," Peta said. "That is what Blossom said. They sent Griffin and he didn't find a trace of Ash anywhere."

I gripped the haft of my spear a little harder. I knew Peta didn't actually know anything more than me. But I needed to ask the questions out loud because if they reverberated inside my head any louder, or longer, I would surely go mad with the sound of them.

With the battle over and the world safe, I had no distraction when it came to him. No reason to not think about him and where he was.

We approached the Rim from the eastern edge. I paused for a moment, running my hands over the trees. This was where my first challenge as an Ender had started. The eastern Rim carried a deadly lung burrower that spread through our Terraling family like a wildfire in the heat of summer. We'd lost at least half our family, and all the trained Enders. The only ones left had been Ash, Blossom, a few other trainees, and myself.

"The past, I see it in your face and feel it through our connection," Peta said. "One day, you will have to let it go."

She was right. I knew she was. Yet I couldn't help but

wonder what would have happened to our world if I'd not been pushed to the limit of my abilities. I shook my head. None of that mattered now. Peta was right; it was time to put the past behind me for good.

I picked up my pace. First to the Rim to check in with Bella and make sure she was safe. She would have info on Ash's last whereabouts, I was sure. Or maybe Griffin would have something, a lead for me to go on.

Then I would be off to find Ash, wherever he was. With my goals set firmly in my mind, I felt my heart settle into an easy rhythm. The Rim was quiet this deep in the night. Movement here and there alerted me to the Rim guards, but they saw me and let me pass without question, only tipping their heads and raising their weapons in a silent salute.

Peta was still in her housecat form and she leapt up to me without warning. I scrambled to catch her as she laughed. "We have to work on your reflexes."

"I'm not a cat, Peta."

"More's the pity. Imagine the fun we could have." She winked. I shook my head and walked straight across the main section of the Rim. Houses sat in a two-mile-long narrow oval with the Spiral at the center. The destroyed Enders Barracks—six months after the battle and it stood as it had then; burned out and desolate—sat to one side of the Spiral. The seat of power for Terralings, the Spiral had been my home for a short while as a child. Not that I cared about that anymore, but I needed a place to sleep. With the Enders Barracks burnt out, that left the Spiral or my old home at the far edge of the Rim. I paused, thinking.

A flutter of feathers and the thump of hooves hitting the ground spun me around. I knew only one creature who had a combination of hooves and wings.

The Pegasus stomped his foot, and snorted as he flung his head up and down, which sent his mane flipping about like a spray of water. "It's about time you got here."

"Where have you been, Shazer?" I wrapped my arms around his neck and he dropped his head over my shoulder. The unspoken question was why hadn't he been with us in the battle against the demons.

"I was behind you on your cross-country run, decided you'd come home eventually and . . . I've been looking for him," he said softly. Him. Ash.

I tightened my hold. "Thank you. Have you—"

"No." He stepped back and shook his head. "There's been no sign of him anywhere. It's like he just disappeared."

"That's not possible. Even if he were dead, there would be sign of him," Peta said. I drew in a slow breath. "He's not dead."

Shazer and Peta shared a look I didn't like. As if they were adults and I the child who didn't understand the ways of the world.

"I need to sleep. Then I will start my search for him in the morning. I'm no good to him running on empty." I said.

I turned from my original path to the Spiral, and headed for the western edge of the Rim. I doubted anyone else had taken over my old home. Bella and her daughter, River, had lived in it during my banishment, even though Bella, at the time, was the heir to the throne. Seeing as she'd given birth to a half-breed, people weren't sure if they wanted her as their potential new queen. Even if she'd told them the child wasn't her choice initially, that River was the result of rape, the truth would have made no difference.

With Peta on my shoulder and Shazer at my side, I made my way without incident across the length of the Rim. Which for me was saying something.

My old home was a redwood tree, the apartment fifty feet up the trunk. Using the pulley and weight system, I was at the doorway in a matter of seconds. I glanced down at Shazer. "Are you staying then?"

He wasn't really a familiar, not like Peta. More like a gift from the mother goddess. A tool I was to use to accomplish the tasks she gave me.

"Seriously, you ask me that after I waited around for twenty-five years for you?"

I grinned. "Had to check."

Peta dropped off my shoulder and trotted into the small apartment. "It smells like Bella's perfume."

I drew in a breath. It did indeed. I stripped as I walked toward the bed, dropping clothes and weapons with thuds and clinks, and with each step, I shed some of the anxiety.

I was home. Safe. I would find Ash and we would finally be together. Maybe I would never have a real home again, but I wouldn't be alone.

I hit the big bed and rolled under the covers, burying my face in the thick pillows. Bella's perfume permeated everything, and I let it calm me. As if my sister were here, watching over me. I closed my eyes. Peta curled up with me, and I passed out.

What felt like only a few short heartbeats later, the sun knocked on my eyelids. "Worm shit," I muttered. "I finally get some sleep without dreams and it lasts less time than it takes to close my eyes."

Peta grumbled something about being hungry. I stretched, the luxury of taking my time something I'd not had . . . since before I'd become an Ender over twenty-five years before. I sat up and stared at the place I'd called home.

Women's clothes taken from the human world were strung out everywhere. Jeans, tank tops, shoes, bras and panties. With the clothes were other human trinkets, paintings, makeup, a box of black and white cookies. I smiled and stood, stretching again, feeling each vertebrae in my back pop as I breathed through the movement.

From behind me came a nicker. I spun to see Shazer curled up on what was a new addition since I'd lived here: a wide balcony. He flipped his lips at me and nickered again. "Nice view."

I rolled my eyes and picked up my clothes, putting them back on, piece by piece. They were also human clothes, but at least they fit: jeans, T-shirt, and sports bra. That would change once I was back in the Spiral. They would have extra clothes for me. Ender clothes.

I tied my long hair in a loose ponytail and headed for the front door. I caught a glimmer of my reflection in a full-length mirror. I paused and stared. How long since I'd last seen myself? Almost as many years as I'd been banished.

Six feet tall, blond hair, one eye green, the other gold. I didn't look any older than I had in my late twenties; elementals aged rather well. But at the same time, I didn't recognize myself. The scarring down my one arm where I'd been branded by the lava whip in the Pit, and the subsequent healing from the mother goddess had left a long tattoo. Though it wasn't actually a tattoo, that was the closest word to describe it. Maybe brand would be better. The pattern was simple: a long curving vine of dark green bearing deep purple thorns that dug into my flesh. I ran a finger down it. Sometimes, if I concentrated, I could almost feel the thorns, and with them the heat of the lava whip.

Even with all that, it was my eyes I was drawn to. "How different am I now, Peta, than when you first met me?"

She sat at my feet and her eyes met mine in the reflection. "By the time we were bonded, you were already not the girl who'd started her journey here. And because of that, I cannot say how much you've changed."

I nodded. "Doesn't matter." But a part of me thought it did. What I'd screamed into the storm stuck with me. I was no longer that wide-eyed girl who'd left the Rim in search of a cure for the lung burrowers. I was no longer the girl who'd fought Requiem in the Deep. Or the girl who'd faced Fiametta in the Pit. Or the girl who so badly wanted her father's love and acceptance.

That girl . . . she was the core of me, but she was weak. And I knew better than anyone that weakness killed faster than a bolt of lightning while you stood in a mud puddle.

"Let's go see Bella." I scooped my toes under the haft of my spear and flipped it up. Before I could catch it, Peta shifted, jumped into the air and caught it with her mouth. She spit it out to me and I caught it.

"Reflexes like a cat," she said. "You should work on that."

Laughing, and knowing that was her intention with her antics, I nodded. "I'll do that."

CHAPTER 3

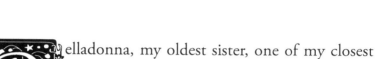

elladonna, my oldest sister, one of my closest friends and now queen of the Rim, stood in nothing but the skin she was born in while a seamstress measured her.

"Ow, do you have to pull so hard?" She glanced down at the older elemental at her feet as she pulled a skirt tight around her waist, tugging at it to get it to overlap further. The seamstress was chunky, like a ball with legs, her body fluffed out like her namesake. Peony, if I recalled right. Only once had she measured me for a custom dress. When I was ten, right before my mother was killed. She'd called me a bastard half-breed and spat at my feet.

"Your Highness, I wouldn't have to pull so hard if you didn't insist on trying to fit into clothes you wore when you were sixteen." Peony swatted Bella on the ass cheek. "Now stop squirming. I'd like to be done before lunch."

Bella's jaw dropped and she glanced at me as I stepped

into the room. "Do you see this behavior? This is not how you treat your sovereign."

I shrugged. "I'd have done worse than swat you on the ass. Probably would have thrown you into a mud puddle."

The seamstress laughed around a mouthful of pins. "I always liked you, Lark. You say what you mean."

I felt the lie as easily as if I'd put my hand out and touched it. One of the perks of having Spirit as an element—or downsides, depending how you looked at it—was that from time to time, I could pick up on the truth of someone's words.

"Oh, I doubt you ever liked me. I am the half-breed bastard, after all," I said softly. The seamstress stiffened and her movements became hurried.

Bella tipped her head to one side. "Really, Lark? Did you have to say that?"

I shrugged. "I can't abide lies, Bella. They soothed me for too many years to swallow them now."

Peony finished and left at a pace that belied the size of her belly. I watched her go, wondering what it said about me that I didn't feel bad for embarrassing her.

Bella snagged a dress and pulled it over her head. "Since you scared Peony away, you have the honor of lacing me up."

I stepped up behind her and took hold of the laces at the back of the dress. Working them quickly, I made sure to pull evenly on each side, her shape forming nicely under the material. "I don't think you've changed since you were sixteen."

"I've had a child, Lark. Of course I've changed." She smoothed her hands over her hips and flat belly. "But you didn't come to talk about the size of my rear, did you?" Her eyes met mine in the reflection of the mirror.

I finished lacing her dress, tying a perfect bow at the top. "No, I didn't."

"What then? You have been home for only a few hours and I see the restlessness in you already." Bella turned and motioned toward a table and two chairs. I sat and immediately stood back up, unable to hold still. She was right, I had to keep moving.

Bella raised both eyebrows, but made no further comment on my inability to sit still. "Wherever you are wanting to go, Lark, you must do it without the armbands."

That stopped me mid-pace. Did she mean to forbid me to leave? Anger swelled and with it, Spirit rose in me, wrapping itself around my connection to the earth. The Spiral shook, trembling.

"Easy, Lark," Peta murmured. "This is your sister, not some errant elemental who wishes you harm."

I kept my mouth shut and waited for Bella to explain, hoping Peta was right.

Bella poured herself a cup of tea, stirred in sugar and cream, and took a sip, acting as though she didn't feel the tremor in the Spiral.

As if she thought the waiting was hard for me.

"I sat in an oubliette for a long time, Bella." I crossed my arms. "I think I can outwait you on a simple explanation."

She grimaced as if her tea were sour. "Goddess, I am an ass. Lark, I'm sorry. The games I must play to keep those around me believing me to be a good queen . . . they never stop. I had no idea."

"You have been queen for only a few months," I pointed out. She'd officially taken the role right before the battle with the demon horde, when our family had turned to her.

Her eyes flashed. "You think it was an easy task you pawned off on me?"

"It was never meant for me, despite what Father said. I am not a Terraling through and through. I cannot abide my feet to be in one place; you said it yourself. You, on the other hand, have always been ready to be the queen." I pointed a finger at her. "You have it in you to be the greatest queen the Rim has seen. I know it."

A tear welled and fell from one of her eyes, plunking into her tea. "Nothing has gone right, Lark. From the beginning. We lost people in the battle against the demons, and when we came back, there was dissent over whether I should be allowed to stay on the throne. Our people have been ruled by so much madness, they are no longer afraid to stand up to their ruler."

I crouched in front of her. "Are our people that malcontent? Perhaps this is perception on your part?"

She closed her eyes and put a hand to her forehead. "Perhaps. The Traveling bands stopped working immediately after we returned. They all said it was the curse of the mother goddess, that she was angry I was on the throne and not another."

Peta slipped up beside us and put her paws on Bella's knees. "Who did they think should take the throne? None of them would want Lark."

"Thanks for the reminder," I snorted.

Bella smiled, but it slipped away. "They want a new family to take the throne. They say ours is so rotten, so corrupted, that we should be cast out."

That didn't sound right. "Bella, are you sure?"

She stood so quickly, she tipped her tea off the table, and if not for Peta's reflexes, she would have had a hot tea bath. "I hear them, Lark. I hear them." She spun the large emerald stone on her middle finger. The stone allowed the wearer to connect with the power of the earth, and in the case of an elemental who already had a connection to the earth, boosted that power tenfold. It had started out as a necklace when I gave it to Bella all those years ago. Somewhere along the line she'd had it reset as a ring.

I put a hand over hers, the bump of the emerald she wore, underneath my fingers. "Be calm, Bella. I doubt this is as bad as you think. I will help you, you know that."

She jerked her hand away from me and clutched her fingers to her chest. "I know nothing of the sort."

What had come over her?

"Ask your question." Peta pressed her head into the back of my calf as if to urge me forward.

Bella glanced at her, whatever anger she'd had, gone in the blink of an eye.

"What question?"

Strangely enough, it took me a moment to gather the words. "Do you have any idea where Ash might be? He was not at the battle. I know you lifted the banishment on him but . . ."

Her eyes widened and then closed in a soft flutter of her lashes. "Oh, Lark. I thought . . . I thought you knew."

My heart thumped hard against my ribcage as I struggled to breathe. "Tell me."

She held a hand out and took mine as I'd done for her only a moment before. My hands were suddenly cold, icy in her warm grip. I couldn't move. I wanted to, but my feet seemed rooted to the floor.

"I sent Griffin to find him, you know that much?" I nodded and she continued. "When he came back, Griffin that is, he . . . I told him to spread the rumor that Ash had not been found. That he was missing. I didn't want—"

"Spit it out." I bit out the words, feeling the pressure

growing behind my eyes, and deep inside my belly. My heart cracked.

"Ash was killed. Cassava did it. He'd been hunting her, we knew that . . . Griffin found her and she gave him Ash's body. We buried him here in the Rim."

For me. Ash had been hunting Cassava for me. After I'd destroyed the Eyrie, Cassava's body had never been found. I knew she was out there, Ash did too.

I reeled away from my sister, the room swirling. The dreams I'd been building, dashed on a single word. Buried. They'd buried him, he was dead. Gone.

"No." I refused it, as if a single denial would make it not so.

"Lark, I am so very sorry."

I stumbled away from her, rushing from the room, blinded by pain that rocked the very center of who I was. I was outside, and without thought I ran to the place that meant the most to Ash, and because of that, to me.

The Enders Barracks.

Though it was a burnt-out shell, the air still filled with the scent of charred wood and leather, I didn't care. It was Ash's home.

My home.

Distantly I knew Peta was with me, even though she didn't speak. I felt her pain with my own. When I'd been in the oubliette the first time, she and Ash had been companions as they'd hunted for me. I knew she loved him, could feel it. I scooped her up in my arms and fell to my knees. The wood below me groaned, and a puff of ash whooshed into the air but the ground held.

A set of arms wrapped around me and I stiffened. I jerked my head up. "Cactus—"

"I heard about Ash," he said softly. "I'm sorry, Lark. I know you cared for him."

His words were conciliatory, but the look in his eyes was barely disguised happiness.

I snapped a fist forward into his nose. "You *are* an ass, Prick. Get the hell away from me."

He fell back with a yell, clutching his nose as blood poured around his fingers. "What is wrong with you, Lark? I tell you I'm sorry you lost a friend—"

"Worm shit! You're damn happy he's gone. You think with Ash dead, you can just move right into my bed? You're out of your ever-loving mind! He was not just my friend, I love him." I stood and pressed the back of one hand to my mouth. I shook all over, the adrenaline and anger, grief and pain mingling into a dangerous blend of energy.

With a quick turn, I had my back to him and strode away, deeper into the burnt barracks. Ash's bedroom wasn't far from the main training area. Maybe there was something remaining of it. Something he'd left behind for me.

Hope flared and fled just as quickly when I stepped into Ash's room. The walls were black, the bed a bare pile of cinders. Even with Peta beside me I struggled to not break down. "Nothing. There is nothing of him left."

"That is not true." Peta swiped at some of the char on the floor in front of her. "You know that. He is in your heart, and as trite as it may seem to say right now, he is safe there. As are your mother and little brother."

"I do not want any more people in my heart. I want them in my life." I brushed a hand over the wall; it came away black. I scrubbed it over my jeans, leaving a long dark smear.

Ashes to ashes, dust to dust. My heart shriveled.

Peta grabbed my lower leg with one paw. "You are filthy. I think it is time to get you cleaned up." She tugged me backward and I went with her, though there was no real contest between us when she was in her housecat form. I followed her out of the room and into the main training area. Cactus was gone.

"Small mercy," I mumbled.

Peta glanced at me, but kept moving. "There is a hot spring under the Spiral, is there not?"

She'd been there. But I knew what she was doing, forcing me to respond to a question we both knew the answer to. Forcing me to pull myself out of the mire, at least a little bit.

"Yes." My lips were numb and even that single word was difficult. Ash was gone. Would I have not felt his passing? Would my heart not have cried out as its other half was stripped from the world? I could not believe he was dead, refused to. Even though there was no reason for Bella to lie. No reason to think Griffin would mislead her. There was a body. They'd buried him.

But still, I couldn't believe it.

"The hot spring is for healing, is it not?" Peta said as she led the way into the Spiral. The guards at the front wouldn't make eye contact with me, not that I cared. I could barely move my legs, as if I'd been drugged. As if everything I'd faced in the last twenty years had finally come home to roost.

The pain, fear, and loneliness, the hope that kept me moving, was gone. Whatever motivation I had to fight was swept away in those few words Bella uttered.

I stumbled down the long stairwell that led to the hot spring, the torches on the side wall flickering as I passed. I stared at the flame, thought of Cactus, and even my anger

48

with him and his selfishness was a mere spurt before it was swallowed in my misery.

My bare feet hit the fine sandy beach and I went to my knees. Peta was there in an instant, her head tucked under my chin, her paws on my chest. "Lark, into the water. Let the heat soothe some of this ache. Besides, you stink."

I blinked down at her. "I stink?"

"Horrible. How long were you in that oubliette? Have you bathed since you got out?" Her words were mundane, the everyday tasks of life. Forcing me to be aware.

"I haven't."

"I can tell." She butted me again under the jaw. "Strip and get in that water."

I did as she told me, peeling the clothes from my body one by one, shedding them with an almost painful slowness.

Naked, I stepped into the shallows, the heat enough to pink my skin immediately. I kept moving until the water reached my waist. Taking a breath, I dove in, the liquid heat rushing over my head. With big strokes, I drove my body through the water, deeper, closer to the source of the heat until it was too much, my body crying out for the cool brush of air. Rolling in the water, I swam toward the surface.

Stroke after stroke, I should have been at the surface already. A strange sense of detachment rolled over me as I realized someone was trying to kill me. I didn't care. Ash was gone and it was the final loss . . . I no longer cared what happened to me.

Peta. Her panic lit a fire in me, and I drove my body forward through the water. I would not give up, if not for myself, then for her. Ash was my love, of that there was no doubt. But Peta was my soul, and I would not leave her behind. A current, like a pair of hands, wrapped around me and drew me down to the source of the heat. I didn't close my eyes, didn't stop swimming, but the dark water blurred my vision, the heat seared my lungs as I could no longer hold out, but drew in a breath.

Flipped upside down, I broke through the surface of the water, coughing, vomiting the fluid in my lungs. The cries of seabirds called to my ears and the cool ocean waves lapped against my skin. Crawling forward, I made it to the edge of the water before I looked up.

I knew what I would see. I was just putting off the inevitable. The woman in front of me looked like my mother, Ulani, with her long blond hair and blue eyes, trim body and faintly pale blue gown. Though it was just a mask, a covering for the woman she truly was.

My eyes met hers. "Hello, Viv."

The mother goddess smiled back, her eyes full of a soft sorrow. "Hello, Larkspur. Are you ready to save the world one more time?"

CHAPTER 4

I curled my fingers into the wet sand, but felt no thrumming power of the earth respond to my call.

"Here, I rule, Lark. You cannot touch your powers unless I allow it." She crouched in front of me. "I know you are hurting, child. I know you think I have betrayed you. I know all these things. But you see only the trees in front of you, not the forest as it spreads around you, as it threatens to swallow you whole."

"You think that because you see everything, and I can't, I shouldn't grieve for him?" I stayed where I was, the water lapping at my feet and legs. I wasn't sure if she was deliberately trying to piss me off, but if she was, it was working.

"Grief," she tucked her fingers under my chin, forcing my head back at a sharp angle, "it is a tool like every other emotion." Her eyes became thoughtful. "I have grieved for thousands of years, for things my children have done. For what they have become. And now . . . I have one last task to ask of you."

The last time I'd seen Viv, I'd told her to get stuffed. That she was asking for my help told me volumes. "Blackbird turned on you, didn't he?"

Her eyes flicked to me and away. "No. But I cannot trust him. Both sides of my nature realize he is . . . unstable. And for what I have need of, unstable is the last thing that would help. He has gone his own way, and I feel that is best."

"A task? I thought you wanted me to save the world?" The bitterness flowing over my words didn't escape me as I settled onto my heels, so we both crouched at the edge of the water.

"A task that would save the world, and one that I wished would never come to light." A heavy sigh slid out of her. "I'd hoped this day was never to be seen by any but in their darkest nightmares. I'd hoped I'd never have to see my children fall so far, but it seems this is my fate. And yours." Her blue eyes narrowed. "Will you listen to my plea?"

The mother goddess had never been so . . . thoughtful when it came to demanding I do something. Or manipulating me into the things she'd wanted me to accomplish. I wasn't sure I liked this new side of her any better.

I dug my toes into the sand, thinking. If she needed my help, and was willing to be gracious, listening was the least I could do.

"I'll listen."

She stood and held a hand out to me. I didn't take it, but stood on my own. Her lips tightened, then smoothed. "You do not have to always be stubborn, child."

Her words were too much like Cactus's for my liking.

My lips tightened, mimicking hers. "I've had too many

hands held out to me in friendship and help that have turned into venomous snakes."

With a deep breath, she nodded. "That is true, forgive me. Walk with me, Lark."

We started down the beach. I couldn't help glancing back. There was no sign of the hot springs I'd left, no sign of Peta coming after me.

The mother goddess held her palm out to me, fingers spread wide. "You know of the five stones, Lark. You have handled them all at one point or another."

I said nothing and she went on. "They were not designed to be held by elementals; they are far too powerful when added to power an elemental already has. Designed to be held by humans, the stones will drive those elementals who hold them tightly, mad."

Bella's strange behavior reared its head and I gritted my teeth. I knew something had been wrong, something that had nothing to do with Bella.

The mother goddess glanced at me. "I see it in your face. You have witnessed this already?"

"Bella."

Her chin dropped to her chest. "She will be the easiest to take the stone from, I believe. She's not held it very long."

"I gave it to her over twenty-five years ago."

She shook her head. "Belladonna has kept the emerald stone locked away. It has only been since the battle with the demons that she's worn it."

The tension across my shoulders eased. "Why would the stone drive her mad?"

The mother goddess pursed her lips, and her eyes grew thoughtful before she spoke. "The stones were created to defend the human world against the elementals. They are imbued with a sentient power that will always seek to battle other elementals." She looked at me as if I could fill in the pieces.

"So the more Bella wears it, the more aggressive she will become? Toward other elementals?" Another thought hit me. "And that is the real reason you won't send Blackbird, isn't it?"

"Yes. Bella will turn on her own people, but more, she will turn on the other families. She will become suspicious, paranoid. It is partly what hurried Cassava's downfall. Not only the use of Spirit, which can be deadly in and of itself to those uninitiated," she gave me a heavy look, "but the property within the stone itself wreaks havoc on the soul."

She paused and clasped her hands in front of her. "And yes, that is another reason I will not ask Blackbird to help me. He would as soon use the stones for his own gain, which I have already seen. He would be . . . far too deadly to have his hands on them. I believe he may be hunting for them too."

And there it was, the real reason she needed my help. "You helped make him what he is, telling him he was your chosen one. Now, he's a menace."

She touched my arm where the mark of the vine and thorn rested. "Which is why you must get to the stones first. You are not like him, Lark. You do not want power; you do not want to rule. I should have seen from the beginning that you were the better choice. Unlike your brother, you always try to make things right. He only wants things the way he sees fit."

Her trust warmed me and I fought the desire to please her. While she was the mother goddess, we had not seen eye to eye for a long time. "Has he retrieved any of the stones?" My mind raced ahead to the possibilities.

"No. You have time yet. Not much, but time nonetheless." A soft smile worked over her lips. As if I'd already said yes, which just pissed me off. I folded my arms and tipped my chin up.

"From Bella, I could take the stone, but why would I bother with the others? That won't save the world. It may save the other families, but I rather doubt the world will miss them."

The mother goddess stopped and put her hands on my shoulders. "Blackbird has lost his mind; the use of Spirit has broken him. He plans to rend the world in half when he gathers the five stones. Lark, he will destroy the entire world. And he would be strong enough with the stones to do it."

I stopped breathing, stood there with no air as her words burrowed into me until I was forced to suck in a breath. "That is not possible."

She nodded. "It is, and he is nearly strong enough to do it on his own. With the stones, it would be a sure thing."

Truth, her words had the ring of truth, and I hated it. "I saw him at the battle. He was not mad."

Why in the seven hells was I defending him?

"I know you don't want to believe it possible." She reached out and took one of my hands in hers. "He does not hide his desires from me. Between his mother, the way she twisted him, and the power he's wielded from a young age, he is not sane. Even if he seems to be." She shook her head and a heavy sigh slipped out of her. "Lark, please—"

"Why don't you get them yourself?" I brushed her hands off mine. "You are the mother goddess. Go to your rulers, take the stones back. You don't need me to do it."

Anger flashed across her face, a dark shadow that was there and gone so fast I almost missed it.

"I cannot. I must follow my own rules. I must not interfere directly with my children's lives. It is impossible. I must work through those I have chosen to speak for me. Those I trust to accomplish tasks I am unable to do. That is why you must do this. This is a task only you can accomplish." She spun, her long braid whipped out around her, and for a moment I could believe she was my mother in truth.

No, I pushed that thought away. That was the kind of thinking that would leave me vulnerable to her demands. I couldn't help myself with what spilled out of me next. Cactus was right. I was too stubborn for my own good, even if I would never admit it out loud.

"And if I say no? What then?"

Her shoulders drooped. "There will be no 'then.' You and Blackbird are the only ones strong enough to take the stones from the other rulers, Lark. If you will not, he will, and then we will all die." She looked over her shoulder, and her face blurred. The ocean tugged at my feet, pulling me back though I held my ground.

"I did not say I would do it!" I yelled at her.

"The child of golden hair, you know of the one I speak?" she called to me, her voice curling through my mind as the scene before me faded. "The child that would have been yours had you stayed in the Rim, and not done as I'd asked. He can still be yours, Lark. But not if you fail in this. Not if the world is destroyed."

The child . . . the child that would have been Ash's and mine.

The implication was as clear to me as a reflection in a mirror polished to a high sheen.

Ash was alive.

"This is the last task I would ask of you, child of mine. The final journey, and you will be free to live your life however you choose, with whomever you choose." Her final words were the clincher. Damn her for striking to the core of me. The ocean water warmed until I was no longer shivering but fighting to get away from the heat. The bright sun cutting through dimmed to mere flickers of torchlight beckoning me to the surface.

I burst out of the water of the hot spring, gasping for air. A spotted snow leopard surfaced beside me, bedraggled and frantic, her green eyes wider than I'd ever seen before they narrowed to mere slits.

"Lark! You're going to be the death of me!" She made as if to swat me and I backpedaled. I didn't need any new scars.

"It was not my fault. The mother goddess pulled me under." I took a stroke, heading back to shore. Peta swam beside me, huffing and puffing.

"How long was I under?"

"Ten minutes. The only thing that kept me from losing my mind was that I could sense you. I knew you were alive." Her green eyes stared straight ahead. "I'm too old for this, Lark. My poor heart can't handle the stress."

I laughed and she glanced at me. I reached out to her, pushing her sideways in the water. "Peta, you are hardly old."

She snorted. "I've been through too much and it has aged me. Most of it with you."

"That I would agree with. I've no doubt most of your grays are from me."

"Did you just make a joke?"

"Maybe." I couldn't help it, hope was filling me where the grief had been. A dangerous thing, hope was, but I couldn't stop myself from believing in the mother goddess's words.

We reached the shore and I slogged out. The clothes I'd

shed were filthy, not to mention human clothes, and I left them on the ground, bending only to pick up my spear.

"Lark, what happened? You seem . . . better," Peta said.

"Ash is alive. I'm sure of it." I strode up the stairs, the water beading on my skin and dripping off which left me shivering, but I barely took note of it. Ash was alive, and I would find him.

"Lark, I want it to be true as much as you but—"

"The mother goddess," I struggled with how to explain my certainty. I knew why the mother goddess had done it—she knew me as well as I knew myself. "Just, trust me. Ash is not dead. I think . . . I have to prove it, though. To be sure."

"Why?" Peta padded along beside me. "Why do you have to prove it?"

My jaw ticked. "I won't take Viv at her word, I can't trust her. This could be another game, another manipulation. But how the hell do I prove he isn't dead?"

Peta paused at the top of the stairs and I stopped with her. She tipped her head to one side. "I saw . . . an old charge of mine delve a grave once using Spirit. He said he could tell if the person was the person actually in the grave or not."

Two guards went by as I stood there, breathing hard, soaking wet, completely naked. Their eyes widened. I didn't recognize either of them. "What are you looking at?"

The one on the left grinned. I pointed my spear at him. "One wrong word, boy, and I'll see you on latrine duty for the rest of your life."

His grin faltered. "I was going to tell you where to find clothes."

"I know where to find the damn clothes," I snapped and strode away. Other Terralings all but leapt out of my way as I headed toward the kitchen. Not that the kitchen was where the clothes were, but the storehouse off to the side was.

The kitchens were quiet this time of day, and I wasn't stopped as I headed for the storeroom.

Everyone knew who I was, and my reputation for destruction. For once, it played in my favor to be known as a bad ass.

Clothing was a necessity, but it took all I had not to rush out to the graveyard on the southeast side of the Rim. I hadn't been there in years, not since my mother and brother were laid to rest.

The storeroom held several sets of Rim Ender uniforms. The leather vest and snug-fitting dark brown pants were tucked away at the bottom of a chest. I pulled them out. The vest I chose had a score mark across the chest. I ran a finger over it. "This was Ash's."

"Are you sure?"

"When we were in the Pit the first time, he got this mark from our first fight with the other Enders." I pulled the vest on, lacing the sides up so it fit me. Pants next and then a leather belt that I hung two smaller bags from. I turned, and Peta sat in the doorway, blocking my way.

"Peta, move."

"Not until you tell me what the mother goddess asked of you. She gives nothing free, Lark. I know that." Her green eyes narrowed.

"Not here. I will tell you, but not here."

"What if she is wrong? What if he is dead? Have you thought that through?" She followed me out of the storeroom and up the stairs.

"Yes. No. I don't know, Peta. I will not even consider that she is wrong at this point."

"That is dangerous," Peta shook her head, "but I understand."

I dropped a hand and ran it down the length of her back. "Thank you, my friend."

We hurried and were outside of the Spiral in a matter of minutes. I took a deep breath, drawing in the smells around me. Redwoods, ferns, budding flowers, the smell of someone cooking. This place should have felt like home. Yet I knew it wasn't, not really. Not anymore.

Home was wherever Ash was.

Someone bumped me from behind and I spun, instantly angry, expecting Cactus. Shazer snorted on me, snot flying from his flaring nostrils. "Lark, I have been looking for you. We must talk. There is something I have to tell you."

I placed a hand on his neck. "Yes, we will talk. But not right now."

His dark eyes narrowed and he pawed at the earth. "When?"

"Soon, just not right now."

"It's important."

Peta shook her head. "She won't hear you no matter how important you might believe it is. There is a chance Ash is alive."

His head snapped up. "Truly?"

"Yes." Just the one word and I was off and running. Through the Rim with Shazer galloping alongside my left, and Peta flanking me on my right. Running with those I trusted, feeling their heartbeats and strength roll through me.

I would need it all if I were wrong, if the mother goddess was wrong, and I had to fully accept that Ash was dead and gone. I slid to a stop at the edge of the Terraling graveyard, my feet suddenly leaden.

The edges were hugged with blackberry vines, thick and tangled, fifteen feet high and curled around the trees. The only opening lay in front of me, an archway of vines. Blackberry blossoms filled the gaps between thorn and vine, a promise of life to come.

I took one step and paused. There was someone already in the yard, someone I did not expect in the least. The man who'd caused me more grief and pain than any other, the man I still wanted to be what I'd imagined as a little girl. My hero, the one who would love me unconditionally, the one who would protect me. Instead he'd become one of my greatest opponents, casting me into the oubliette the second time as though I were trash to be buried and forgotten.

My heart beat harder, thumping and fighting as if it would leap out of my chest. I loved him as much as I hated him, and I did not know if I could reconcile the two emotions. Not now certainly, and maybe not ever.

"Isn't that . . ." Peta whispered.

"Yes," I nodded. "That's my father."

CHAPTER 5

The former king of the Rim sat on a stone bench next to a grave I knew all too well, a red hawk on his shoulder I also knew rather well.

My mother had been buried in the center of the graveyard, as a place of honor. To her left rested Bramley, a sleeping baby forever. For just a moment, I saw his smiling, laughing face and chubby cheeks, his bright eyes. The way he'd clung to me in his last moments.

Old grief, pain I thought I'd left behind curled up and cut through the hope that had buoyed me. I put a fist to my belly, doing what I could to quell the roll of emotions.

"Shazer," I put a hand on his neck, "stay at the gate, keep watch."

He snorted and bobbed his head as I stepped through the archway. Peta kept tightly to my side, her unwavering support about all that kept me moving through the memories that surrounded me, filling my mind and making my steps slow.

The hawk turned, saw me and tipped his head in acknowledgment. Red had been my companion in the desert, not that he'd wanted to be there. But as one of my father's three familiars, he'd been sent to watch over me.

I lifted a hand to him. I would not slight him. He was a good familiar, even if he was not one of mine. And he'd helped me, knowing I did what I thought was best and supporting me as much as he was able at the time, even against my father's wishes.

The newest graves were closest to the gate, and if I kept quiet, perhaps my father wouldn't notice me. Though his betrayal was not truly his, with his mind manipulated by Cassava and then Blackbird, I could never truly allow myself to feel for him again. He was just a pitiful old man now, broken and weak, his family lost to him. I refused to let myself believe he would ever be anything else.

I bent beside the grave closest to me. Persimmon, Simmy, my old friend from the planting fields. She'd died when the lung burrowers had gone through our family, and her daughter blamed me.

Another old hurt; I'd not saved more of my family.

I moved past her grave and to the next and the next, until I came to the far right side of the graveyard. I glanced over at my father. He was still oblivious to my presence. That or he was ignoring me.

Enough stalling. I looked at the grave I'd come to see. Against the thorny wall, his name was etched into a flat piece of obsidian.

Ash, loyal Ender of the Rim.
Rest in the mother goddess's embrace.

My throat tightened and fear made me stumble. He

would not be in the grave, I had to believe. I dropped to my knees, the soft ground giving way with a poof of dust that rose around me. Pausing, I glanced at Peta who hadn't moved from my side.

"You can do this. No matter the outcome, I am here. I am with you." Her words were all I needed. Even if I lost Ash, I had Peta, and she would see me through this darkness too.

Closing my eyes, I buried my hands into the soil of the grave. "I am afraid, Peta. Spirit, you said it is getting wild and—"

"Then do it fast, Lark. Do not hesitate," she whispered.

I opened myself to Spirit and it roared awake, like a beast inside me. It tangled itself with Earth as if it would take hold of my other element again. I held my connection to the earth tightly to me and Spirit slid away and down my arms like nothing more than a petulant child.

But it was not trying to take control, not this time.

Twenty feet deep, Spirit fell and then wrapped around a body. Images and flickers of what Spirit felt came back to me. An Ender vest, a short sword, nothing else. Yet even that was enough to confirm for me that the mother goddess had lied to me yet again.

And her lie broke me.

I couldn't stop the cry that escaped me, the budding hope dashed as though slammed with a sudden frost. A trembling set of hands touched mine.

"Death is not the end, my girl."

I blinked up, and found myself staring into my father's face. He'd aged since I'd seen him last, and not well. He'd not been at the battle against the demons, and now I knew why. His once-robust frame had thinned and become gaunt, his hair had gone completely gray, hanging down in a knotted mess to the middle of his back. But the second his hand touched my skin, his eyes, fogged with confusion, cleared. These were the eyes of the father I recalled from my childhood. Dark forest green and full of kindness, full of strength and wisdom.

A sob escaped me. "I cannot keep losing those I love."

He caught me against his chest, crushing me to him as I'd longed for him to do for years.

No more words passed between us and yet the forgiveness was there. He held me as I sobbed, unable to stop the grief from pouring out of me, finally finding some refuge in my father.

Peta put a paw on my hand, adding to the love that surrounded me.

"Child, why do you grieve so hard?" My father set me back from him but I made sure to keep some contact on his skin.

"Ash, he's in the grave, and I thought maybe . . . maybe he wasn't." Stupid, stupid words, I couldn't help them.

Red fluttered his wings. "There are more ways than one to find out if the body is truly that of Ash."

Basileus frowned. "Red is right. If there is any doubt, bring the body up."

I swallowed hard. "I do not know if I could stand seeing him half eaten by worms."

My father nodded. "That I understand all too well. I brought your mother up not long after she was buried. I couldn't believe she was gone, I had to see her with my own eyes again." He grimaced, pain shooting across his face like a falling star. "While it was one of the most difficult things I have done, it allowed me to move on."

I bit back the retort that perhaps instead of moving on he should have killed the one who'd murdered my mother.

I kept a hand on him.

"Lark." He smiled at me. "You are so like your mother. When she put her hand on me, my mind cleared, just like now."

I gave him a smile, though it slid from my face quickly. "Basileus. When I let go of you, I want you to go back to the Spiral. Please."

"I have to tell you something first." He leaned in close to me, so our foreheads touched. "There is a story I remember from when I was very, very small. Barely to my mother's knees. Whispers of a legend I didn't recall until now, yet I think you must hear it."

I wasn't sure what to think. Was it a true clearing of his mind or had he slipped further into his madness? I glanced up at Red who ruffled his feathers. "I've not got a clue of what he speaks."

My father touched my face, drawing my attention back to him. "A legend, a story. That the mother goddess we know, she is not what she seems. That she is . . . mortal, like we are. Long-lived, but mortal, a wolf in sheep's clothing."

I blinked several times, his words settling in my head. "That is not possible, Basileus. She is the mother goddess, I have felt her power."

He tightened his hold on my face, breathing shallow gulps. "I am not long for this world and I would tell you this. I am one of the oldest of any elemental left. I have seen rulers come and go. I waited until I thought the world was safe to have my children, and even now they are torn from me, killed by each other and by themselves."

I gritted my teeth, knowing I was one of the reasons his children had been harmed.

"Basil—"

"No, I have to say it." His eyes were intense and he didn't

blink once. "I believe the legend; the mother goddess is not a goddess. She is an elemental. Like you and me and all the others. And she will destroy you if she can. I have seen in her mind, in my madness I have walked with her. She will make Cassava look like the sweetest peach in the garden if you see the truth of what she is."

His words shivered along my spine, but I knew them for what they were. Madness, pure and simple.

I looked again to Red. "You've been with him a long time, my friend. What say you?"

Red shook his head, his eyes sad. "It is as you fear: madness. I stay with him now out of loyalty. The other two have disappeared."

The other two. Red had to mean the bear shifter, Karhu, and the husky, Hercules. I let go of my father, and kissed him on the forehead. "Go to the Spiral. I cannot be sure you will be safe when I bring up the body." I couldn't say *his* name, even now. Ash's body. That was what I would raise, not the man I loved.

My father's eyes fogged and he looked around him. "The darkness climbs the vine, closing in on the blooms and the flower petals drop in decay to the ground once more."

A cool breeze accompanied my father's words, blowing through my hair in a whisper that almost echoed what he'd said. I shook off the sensation. There was no room for fancy in this world of ours.

"Come on, old man. Let's find a place to sleep the day away." Red flew into the air and a long trailing rope hung from his claws. Father reached up and took hold of the rope and Red led him away from the graveyard.

I watched them go, knowing I was stalling.

"Lark, you will not rest until you see his body in the

flesh. I know you well enough to know that is the truth." Peta touched the headstone with Ash's name engraved with her nose.

I went to my knees to one side of the grave. The last thing I wanted was an explosion of power when bringing a partially decayed body out of the ground. I swallowed hard and gently called the power of the earth to me. Within the power, I wove all the love I had for Ash, the hope that he was alive, and the belief I knew he'd always had in me.

Spirit flowed with it, quiet, reverent in its feel against me.

The ground shimmied and shifted under my hands, shaking like a giant flour sifter until the shape of a body began to emerge. My hands trembled as the dirt slid from his face. I gasped and let go of the power under me. Brushing the dirt off the face, the features emerged; high cheekbones, delicate bone structure, tiny ears; it wasn't Ash.

It was a woman.

A cry escaped me and I raised my hands over my head as relief flowed through me, hope growing in leaps and bounds once more.

Ash was not dead . . .but then why would Bella say he was? Did she not know either that the body was not his?

Peta seemed to read my mind. "Someone using Spirit could have made this body look like Ash's. I doubt your sister, or even Griffin knew that it wasn't him."

I sat there staring at a new reality I'd have never have thought possible. As long as his heart beat, I could find him. We could make a life together. There was a chance that all we'd faced would be over soon.

Sobbing, I slung an arm around Peta. "He's alive, he's alive."

"You can find him. I know you can," she whispered through her own tears. "If anyone can make this right, you can."

We clung to each other for a few minutes before I got control of myself. I let Peta go, and took a deep breath. "I'll put her back, then we'll go see if—"

Peta leaned forward. "Oh, that can't be good."

I followed her gaze and looked down at the body in the shallow grave.

Clutched in the woman's hands was a tiny box with . . . my name on it.

I brushed a hand over the box and the woman's fingers clenched it. I scrambled back, my heart rate flying to the tops of the redwoods around us.

"Worm shit."

Peta crouched beside me, her body quivering. "Is it a booby trap?"

Damn it, I should be smarter than this. But the idea that Ash was alive had made me reckless and stupid. Blackbird knew me too well, he'd done this.

On my belly, I crept toward the partially covered body. The fingers clenched the box until the wood creaked. Her body arched so she was raised on her heels and the back of her head. Her mouth opened, dirt falling into her gaping maw.

"Laaaaarkspuuuuuuur."

A snarl rolled out of Peta and I waved a hand at her. "Stay back."

The body twitched and rolled, until the empty eye sockets faced me. The only thing I could think was that at least it wasn't someone I recognized, a nameless face. Small comfort when looking into the eyes of the dead come to life.

Her jaw opened and closed. The gritty sound of dirt grinding on her teeth made me flinch.

"Taaaaake iiiiiit." She held the wooden box out to me.

Peta shook her head, reached and grabbed at my arm with her big paw. "Don't, you don't know—"

She was right, I didn't know what was waiting for me. "What if it's something from Ash? A hint about where he is?"

Peta's paw slid off me. "I don't like this."

Swallowing hard, I held my hand out and the corpse dropped the box onto my hand. I pulled away, sliding across the dirt and graves until I was the length of a sapling away from her.

The corpse stayed where she was, staring toward me with her empty eyes, her voice clearing as she spoke, changing into one I knew. "Use the stones within to replace those you take. When it is done, I will help you find your golden eagle."

Golden eagle. Golden-haired child. I knew what the message was; the mother goddess would help me find Ash. Damn her, damn her through all seven levels of hell and back. She'd known I wouldn't be able to resist coming to his grave, to see if he was actually in it.

Apparently she knew me better than I thought.

I flipped the wooden box open without another thought, and sucked in a sharp breath that tasted of dirt and molding death.

Five stones rested within the bare bones box. Emerald, sapphire, smoky diamond, ruby, and pink diamond. One for each of the five elements. I brushed a hand over them, feeling no connection to any of the elements. Just stones, then.

The corpse lay back, her mouth stopped moving and her body shuddered as she was drawn back into the earth. That was not something I did.

Peta stuck her nose into the box. "Are these what I think they are?"

"Yes, they're fakes to replace the real ones." I slid them into the palm of my hand. They glittered in the sunlight filtering through the trees. I'd held the real ones, and these were perfect replicas, down to the settings. Some were rings, others necklaces. I put them into the leather pouch at my hip and pulled it shut tightly.

"You ready to tell me what the mother goddess had to say, *now*?" Peta asked.

Her sarcasm was not lost on me.

"I'm to steal the stones from the rulers and take them to the mother goddess. Blackbird is hunting for the stones too, and . . . he's lost his mind. If he gets them all, he's going to tear the world apart."

"Why would he do that? What good would it do for him to destroy this planet?" Peta asked. It was a good question.

"Perhaps that is part of losing his mind. Maybe he thinks he is a god now and can remake this world in his own image?" I shook my head. "Does it matter why? I only know that he plans to." Then again, I was going by what the mother goddess told me. Call it a hunch, but I suspected I wasn't yet getting all the truth from her either.

Peta sat on her haunches. Her jaw opened and closed several times, reminding me more than a little of the animated corpse. A shiver of premonition slid over me and I shook it off. There was no way Peta was going to die.

She squinted one eye. "I thought that was just a story."

I stilled. "What do you mean, just a story?"

She hunched her shoulders. "A single line I read when I

was with Talan, years ago. Yet it stayed with me because . . . well—"

I stared at her, fear creeping up my spine. "Just say it."

Her eyes closed and she spoke. "When the world is broken and must be healed, the only recourse is to break it."

I blinked several times. "That doesn't even make sense."

"But if Blackbird read that, could he believe he is saving the world somehow?"

I shrugged. "It doesn't matter what he thinks. The only thing that matters is that we get to the stones before him."

I sat where I was and dusted off my clothes while my mind raced ahead. Planning how I would make each theft happen. To take one stone from a ruler would be hard. To take all four? A near impossible task, because as soon as one was retrieved, I had no doubt the other rulers would be tipped off and be waiting for me. And the fifth stone? That one was hidden away, and I planned to keep it that way until the last possible second. I'd grab it before we left the Rim. At least that was my plan.

Peta looked up at me. "That means you need to take Bella's stone. But she will give it to you if you ask. That, at least, will be easy."

I grunted. "Did I forget to tell you that the longer the rulers hold the stones, the real ones, the crazier they get?"

Peta's eyes fluttered. "Of course they do. Why wouldn't they?"

From the entrance to the graveyard, Shazer snorted, drawing our eyes to him. "Someone comes."

The Pegasus shuddered, his head and wings drooped and his body shivered as he lay down where he was and closed his eyes.

I leapt to my feet. "Shazer?"

I turned, and Peta wobbled where she sat, her eyes

softening as she fell asleep, slumping where she was into a lopsided ball.

The crack of a twig to my left snapped me into action. I grabbed my spear and spun, holding the weapon out in front of me. A man stood against the wall of thorns, his arms folded over his chest, his dark blue eyes thoughtful. He had dark hair that at first I thought was short, until he took a step and I saw the long swing of a braid down his back.

A shiver slid over my skin, the feel of something I knew rather well.

Spirit, he used Spirit on me.

"Why did you down my familiars? Who are you?"

He said nothing to my questions, just watched me as the feeling of Spirit on my skin intensified and I stood, shaking and quivering under it. Wanting more of it, the feeling of Spirit tamed and soothing, the sensation of it lighting up my skin with the faint prickle of electricity.

The flush of desire spread across my skin and I took a step toward him, wanting more of what he offered without a single word. Wanting the peace that exuded from him.

One step and I froze, my own connection to Spirit rising in me, wiping out the control he rolled over me.

What the hell was I thinking? Only moments before all I could think about was Ash, and now this stranger showed up and . . . manipulated me with Spirit. Goose shit, there wasn't even a line of power on his arms. How was he hiding what he did from me?

"You bastard."

He gave me a soft smile, winked, and turned away, seemingly stepping into the thick vines, disappearing without so much as a single damn word.

At my feet, Peta stirred, giving a jaw-cracking yawn. "What happened?"

"Someone . . . knocked you out with Spirit. You and Shazer."

The Pegasus snorted and rubbed his muzzle on the short grass. "Two more minutes, Mom, I'm tired."

I rolled my eyes and started out of the graveyard, only to be stopped by the sight of Red flying through the trees, trailing my father behind him.

"Lark, you must do something," My father called to me, hurrying as fast as he could.

I raised my eyebrows at Red and he slowed as he dropped to my shoulder. "As soon as we left, he started mumbling about the truth, about it being lost, the world twisted by Cassava. Not that those are anything new."

My father drew close to me, his eyes intense. "I remembered what I needed to tell you."

I held a hand out to him. "Tell me then."

He batted my hand away. "Listen to me. Listen to me. Your man was not in the grave."

"No, he wasn't."

He leaned in close, dark green eyes wide. "He is not the only one you love who does not rest in a grave."

CHAPTER 6

hat was I to say to that? "Father, I do not doubt you mean well, but—"

"Of course you don't believe me, but that is fine. You'll see. Come, come to the graves again. I feel them in the earth, all those I've lost. It is a talent I have. But one is missing and I wasn't supposed to remember, and now when you put your hands on me things have come back, a little more, a little more." He rambled as he hurried into the graveyard, pushing me aside in his need to show the truth as he saw it.

I followed him to my mother's grave. My whole body stiffened at the implication. He took my hand and pressed it downward. "What do you feel, deep in the earth?"

Shaking, I did as he asked and delved with Spirit and Earth, feeling the body deep within. A hint of who she'd been flowed up to me and I wondered if it was because she'd carried Spirit too.

"You feel her, don't you? Hear her sing to you," he

whispered. "I hear her call to me. My time to be with her again is soon."

He grabbed my hand and tugged me to the side. "Now, your brother."

I closed my eyes, not in concentration, but because I did not want to feel my little brother. How many years had I dreamt of his death, how many years had I blamed myself for not saving him?

"I don't—"

"Do it, Lark." His command was that of the king I'd known, and I was delving into the earth without another thought, acting before I realized it. Deeper and deeper I went, past the depth of most burials, and then more. My eyes flew open as my power spiked, and Spirit went wild within the earth. The graves around me lit up, a perfect layout of every Terraling ever buried. I felt them against my skin, Spirit opening to me in a way I'd never experienced. But my father was right.

"He's not here," I breathed.

"I know. I know he isn't, but I wasn't supposed to know. I wasn't supposed to remember. Why, why isn't he here, Lark?"

I swayed where I was. "Is he . . . alive?"

Mother goddess have mercy, all these years and I'd never once doubted Bramley's death. How easy would it have been for Cassava to manipulate my mind, to make me see Bramley dead? But that didn't make sense. He'd been her target all along as the heir to the throne. She even admitted it.

Yet her words, the last time we'd battled, came back to me. She'd implied he wasn't dead and I'd chalked it up to her wanting to hurt me. To taunt me with a reality that wasn't possible.

Now I wasn't so sure.

I drew Spirit back to me, damping it down without thought. It went easier than before. Perhaps my grief kept it from being wild.

"I don't know," Basileus whispered. "I don't know. I just know he isn't here. Will you find him, Lark?"

Shaking, I stood and held my hand out to him, pushing all the questions to the back of my mind. "Come, back to the Spiral with you."

Red fluttered down from the edge of the graveyard vines. "I'll take him. He'll go now that he's said his piece."

My father touched my face, and his eyes cleared. "I don't know where he is, Lark. But if he's alive, he needs you."

He dropped his hand, turned, and shuffled away again. I watched him go, my heart hammering, emotions tangling in my throat and belly like a writhing cauldron.

"Peta, how can this be? I held Bramley. I felt his body as still as a doll's." I pressed the heels of my hands to my eyes. "My mind is clear of all the tricks Cassava pulled, all the manipulation. But that scene remains. It happened. I know it did."

"You are sure he is dead?" Peta asked softly, as gently as she'd ever been with me.

Tipping my head back, I stared into the canopy above us, the branches that swayed in the breeze somehow clearing my mind of doubt. "Yes. As much as I wish it were otherwise, I will not be fooled by this trick. But where the hell is he, then? Why would they put his body away from our mother's?"

Shazer trotted in and head-butted my back. "Because it is a distraction. You cannot chase two quests at once. You know Ash is alive. You know Bramley is dead. Who will you choose to find? The one you can save? Or the one you will never save?"

I tightened my jaw, even though a part of me howled to go after Bramley, still seeing him as that little boy from my past. "Ash."

"Then let's go. I have things to tell you that are pertinent." He snorted and shoved me toward the archway.

Peta leapt for his back and he shied to one side. "Claws, cat, you have claws!"

She hit the ground, shifted and sprung again, this time tangling her much tinier paws into his mane. "Sissy."

He grunted. "I'm a delicate flower."

I burst out laughing at their exchange, knowing that was the exact reason they did it. "You two are fools."

Shazer glanced back at me. "You finally have a minute to listen to me?"

I waved at him. "Why not? Can't make things worse, can it?" The look in his dark eyes sent a shiver through me. "Please tell me that things can't get worse."

He slowed and I caught up to his shoulder. "I don't know. Maybe."

I waited for him to speak, feeling time slip past. If the mother goddess was right, I had to get moving and remove the stones from the other rulers; I had no doubt Blackbird would be plotting a way to remove them. Then again, that wasn't really why I was in a hurry. Without Viv's help, finding Ash was going to be damn near impossible and I knew it.

So did she.

Shazer bobbed his head. "You realize I'm not really a familiar to you? That there is a bond between us, but it is not like the bond you and Peta have?"

I nodded. "I noticed the feeling between you and me is different, yes."

"It is because I was created. Peta was born. And I was never truly tied to you. I stay because . . ." His body rippled in a big shake that almost unseated Peta. She grunted and dug her claws in. He snapped his teeth at her before continuing. "I stay because I feel more loyalty to you than I do my creator. Even when you didn't know me, you put your life on the line to heal me; to save me from the coven. That loyalty has grown, even while you were gone. The need to stay with you and protect you as best I could for your sake, and, I think, for my own as well."

"All right," I said, confused as to why this was so important.

He tipped his head. "There is more to it than that. The person who created me also created something else. The stones you are going in search of were made by my creator."

Obviously he'd been listening in on my conversation with Peta. Not that I minded.

"All right."

"He was always hidden in a cloak when around me, not unlike the way that donkey's ass Blackbird covers up. He was cursed, Lark. For the things he created, the things he was powerful enough to do. The Spirit Elementals saw what he was up to, and knew he had to be stopped. They contacted a powerful witch, and they created a curse."

"Why wouldn't they just kill him?" Peta asked the question, beating me to it. I nodded at her in approval.

He shook his head. "He was too strong. There was no one that could stand against him, and even then the elementals were at each other's throats. There was no peace and he took advantage of that rather looming fact." Shazer's eyes went thoughtful as if seeing the past in front of him. "He created the stones first, and they were meant to control others. Out there in the world, they are able to control those who wear them."

I frowned and plucked at a long strand of grass as we approached the Rim. "But that would mean your creator is still alive. And from what I understand, you are rather—"

"Old," Peta spit out.

Shazer snorted and laughed. "Yes, I'm old. Thousands of years, the same as the stones. And my creator is still out there, I am sure of it. Maybe he sleeps, maybe not. But he is alive."

My mind went to the man in the graveyard; he'd plied me with Spirit while he hid his intentions. The timing was far too coincidental for my liking. "Tell me about the curse."

"He's not able to directly attack another elemental. That is why he created the stones. He could use the wearer of them to attack those he thought needed to be punished. I will say this, Lark. If he wakes, he will not be easily dealt with. He is beyond dangerous; he is the deadliest of any elemental ever born."

I swallowed hard. "Why might he wake?"

"If the stones are all brought to him, together, the curse will be broken. And that would be a very, very bad thing. Because then he could attack any elemental directly with no more need to work in the shadows."

We stepped into the Rim as he finished speaking.

Shazer's words were heavy on my mind, adding to the weight on my shoulders. "One more reason then to find the stones and take them to the mother goddess for safe keeping," I said.

He nodded. "Agreed."

Peta bobbed her head too. "Agreed."

So many swirling pieces, it was hard to make heads or tails of what was truly going on.

"As long as we get the five stones first, none of that will matter." Peta swayed on Shazer's back and he glanced at her.

"She's right. Deal with the stones so we can find Ash. Deal with everything else later," Shazer said.

"Nice, we are all in agreement," I mumbled.

I approached the steps of the Spiral and headed up. Peta leapt from Shazer's back. "How are you going to get . . . it . . . from your sister?"

I kept my face smooth. "Simple. I'm going to ask."

"You think it will be that easy?" Peta kept pace at my side.

"Hoping."

Really, how attached could Bella be to the emerald? While the ring had been in her possession for twenty-plus years, she'd only worn it since she'd taken the throne, as the mother goddess had reminded me. Surely a few weeks wasn't long enough for madness to begin.

I chose not to consider her behavior earlier, chalking it up to stress. The soft gong of the dinner bell brought my head around; the day had flown by, my time in the grave taking longer than I'd realized.

"The dining hall then." Even better. Bella was not one to make a scene, so taking the ring would be even easier if I asked for it in a public place. I fished around in my leather pouch as we walked, finding the emerald by feel. I paused and then let it go. There was no need for swapping it out; taking the ring would be as simple as a request.

We approached the open dining hall. Guards stood at the door, but they were relaxed and nodded to me in recognition.

The one on the left gave me a tentative smile. "Will you start the Ender program again, Larkspur?"

Startled by the question, I stopped and faced the guard who'd spoken. "Perhaps. I have tasks ahead of me, but when I am done, it would seem prudent to flesh the ranks out again."

He slipped his helmet off and held out his hand. "Name is Arb. I'd like to take part when you open the training again."

I took his hand and shook it once. "I will let you know."

Stepping through the doorway, I headed straight for Bella, my heart rate climbing with each footstep, tension mounting across my shoulders.

"Peta, be ready."

"I thought you said this was going to be easy?" she whispered.

"Well, this is my family. Who the hell really knows?"

She laughed and I smiled down at her.

"Lark," Bella called to me, laughter in her voice. I looked up and she waved to us. "Come, sit with us, eat with us. Tell us what you've been up to today."

I smiled at her, noting her daughter to her right. River was as stunning as her mother, with her perfect soft curves, high cheekbones, and delicate features. Her coloring, though, set her apart among the other Terralings. As a half-breed, her father's Undine bloodlines showed clearly in her Caribbean blue eyes which were offset by her nearly black hair. Her coloring was not far from Raven's. I had to fight to keep my smile on my face. River waved at me. "Auntie."

The words slowed my feet. Damn, she was my only niece and she'd never called me auntie before. Not that she'd had much choice, it wasn't like I'd been around a lot since she'd been born. I slowed as I approached the table. "Bella, a quick question before I eat."

"Of course." She raised a spoonful of soup to her mouth, the emerald ring glinting on her third finger.

"May I inspect your ring? I am concerned with a flaw in it." The lie was smooth and easy. River didn't look up from her meal; no one took notice. This was going to work.

Bella lowered her spoon and frowned at me. "A flaw? There is no flaw in this emerald. It is perfect."

She dropped her hands to her lap and covered the ring with her other hand. I continued to smile even while the tension grew. "But a flaw in the setting that would allow the stone to fall out would be an easy thing to have fixed."

"Mother, she's right. Let her see it. You'd be frantic if the stone were to go missing," River added absently.

Bella's eyes hardened as she stared at me. "You would take it from me?"

"Of course not," I said, feeling the air between us shift. I held up both hands, palms facing her. "Bella, I would never take it from you."

The moment stretched and I saw her weigh my words.

"Lies," she snapped, suddenly and with such force she actually spit. "You would take it for your own. You want it for yourself." She stood and the lines of power curled around her arms in a slow deadly march. I made myself stand there, made myself allow her to sink me into the ground to my waist. I had to continue the charade that I didn't want the stone.

River stood.

"Mother, what are you doing?"

"She's here to take the throne from me. She has been waiting for this moment." Spit trickled from her lips and my heart clenched. *Mother goddess let me not be too late. Let her not face the same fate as our father.*

"Bella, do not do this." I shifted, pulling on the earth and pushing myself out of the ground.

She circled me, the emerald flashing. "I will make sure there are no threats to this family, however I must. Even if it means your death, Destroyer."

And there it was. Inside my heart, I cried at the loss of my sister. Outside, I gripped my spear and swung it in a low, lazy circle.

"Then come for me, if you dare."

CHAPTER 7

Bella lifted her hands, intent clear as the lines of power raced up her arms. I buried my spear into the ground at my feet.

"Lark, you don't know if you have enough control, you can't use your connection to the earth to fight and be sure you won't topple the Rim." Peta spoke low, but Bella heard.

"You would not fight me? Then you are the fool, aren't you?"

Jaw tight, I reached for the connection to the earth, demanding it bend to me, weaving Spirit around it and boosting the power. The last time I'd faced someone who wore the emerald stone, I'd destroyed the Eyrie. I wouldn't do that here. This was my family's home and I didn't want to kill Bella; I didn't want to hurt her at all.

But I could not leave the emerald with her, that much was obvious. To save her, I was going to have to hurt her. I hardened myself against the grief that would stop me from doing what I must.

I pushed my power into the Spiral, solidifying the cracks Bella tried to exploit. We stood, facing one another as sweat dripped down our faces. She sought to pull the Spiral apart and I patched it together. Back and forth the Spiral groaned, the earth shuddering now and again. To any watching, they would see us in a standoff, but not understand.

I was the only one who could see the lines of power on another's arms.

Peta paced in front of me. "Lark—"

"No, leave her to me," I said through gritted teeth. It wasn't that she was that much stronger than me, but Bella had control and practice with her abilities that I'd never had. I'd never been trained with either Earth or Spirit. I'd always just used sheer strength to overwhelm my enemies.

And for the first time in my life, that truly meant something. I couldn't just overpower my sister. I would end up killing her, which I wasn't willing to do—not even for Ash. Not even to save the world.

But the control it took to chase the destruction she tried to bring down on us was beyond me.

"Give up, half-breed," she snapped, taking a step toward me.

I tapped deeper into Spirit, feeding it into my words. "The ring, Bella, give me the damn ring!"

She wavered, her eyes fogging long enough for me to hope that she would hand it over.

"NEVER!"

So much for that idea. Spirit flowed through me, tugging me in three different directions. I stumbled and went to one knee. The room shook and dust fell from the ceiling as I was pulled away from my connection to the earth, and

Bella ripped at the Spiral without me as an obstacle. Those in the room stood, and a few cried out.

"You have to end this—now." Peta ran across the room, and leapt onto the dining table, right in front of River.

Peta looked at me, then dipped her head to River. I knew what she wanted me to do, and I was loathe to even take that measure.

"And if it doesn't work?"

Peta had no answer, and I knew she was right. The Rim trembled as Bella and I waged a war no one else realized was happening. I had maybe a minute left before I lost control of my power and it ran away with me. I could feel it slipping with each breath I took.

I stood and bolted across the room, leapt up on the table and landed on the other side behind River. "Trust me, niece."

"What?"

I jerked her out of her seat, even as I wrapped my free arm around her neck. I scooped one of the dinner knives from the table and laid it across her throat.

"Your daughter's life for the ring, Belladonna. Now."

Bella's jaw dropped, River drove an elbow back into me, and I pressed hard enough with the knife to draw a thin line of blood, stilling her.

"You wouldn't dare!" Bella snapped. "I see it in your eyes, it is a ruse."

"We have been apart a long time." My voice was deadly soft. "Perhaps you don't know me as well as you think." I took the knife from River's neck and drove it into her thigh, twisting it, cutting through muscle and flesh.

River screamed and convulsed against me, and I whipped the knife back up to her throat. "The ring, Belladonna. Throw it to me."

Bella stared, her eyes wide and glassy.

River sobbed. "Mother, please, give her the ring. Please don't let her kill me."

A tiny piece of me died knowing nothing would ever change River's view of me after this. That I would be the one who haunted her nightmares for years.

Trembling, Bella shook her head. "I—"

I dug the rough, serrated edge into River's collarbone. "MOTHER!"

Bella cried out, ripped the ring from her hand and threw it across to me. I let River go and caught it in mid-air.

River fell to the floor. I could heal her, but I doubted she would let me touch her. Bella ran forward, tears streaming down her face as she sobbed her daughter's name.

River clung to her, then pushed her away. "You would trade my life on a ring."

"She would never have killed you, I—" Bella looked up and I saw my sister in her eyes. The sister I trusted. And so I told her the truth.

"If I had to, I would have."

Bella blanched. "If you had to?"

River's blue eyes were full of fury as they turned to me and for a moment I caught a glimpse of her father in her. I shuddered with that quick reminder of Requiem and the man he was, and answered honestly. "If you had not given me the ring, would you rather I tear the Rim apart and kill many, or kill one and in your grief make you weak enough to take the ring from you?"

Bella's mouth dropped open. "You wouldn't have."

"Yes," I said. "I would have. I know you, Bella. But I do not think you know me any longer."

I hadn't meant to say that, but the words slipped out.

Peta sat quietly beside me. "It is the age-old mistake people make," she said, "believing those we love aren't capable of harming us, and so we trust them."

I grimaced, Peta's words not really helping smooth things over.

Bella called for the guards who slipped in, their heads down. Her eyes on them said it all. Where were they when the fight was going on? Where were they when they should have been protecting their queen? Even though she was in the wrong, they still should have come running to defend her.

"We didn't know you were fighting," young Arb said.

She nodded, her eyes and face softening. "I know. That is no fault of your own. More training I think is needed. We have not had a true Ender for years." Her eyes climbed to mine, shame filling them. "Lark, what happened to me?" The unspoken question with it, what had happened to me as well? Why wasn't I the Lark she remembered? The little sister she remembered.

"I do not think this is a good place to discuss what is going on."

River continued to glare at me through all this. "Mother, you obviously can't trust her, she's dangerous."

With her hand clinging to her daughter's, Bella shook her head. "River, I do not expect you to understand. Despite what your aunt says, I don't believe she would have hurt you."

Wisely, I kept my mouth shut. Because Bella was the one who was wrong. I knew it in my gut: the oubliette had changed me, and I wasn't sure it was for the better.

I motioned for her to follow me. She bent and kissed River on the head. "I will see you at the healers."

"Mother, don't do this, do not trust her. They call her the Destroyer for a reason." River clung to Bella.

Bella took River's hand from hers and smiled. "It will be all right. Trust me, even if you do not trust Lark."

Several tears slid down River's face. "I do not know if I can even do that." She was picked up and carried away to the healers.

If I had stabbed Bella myself, the pain in her face would not have been greater than it was with River's words. She watched her daughter go, tiny shudders crossing her shoulders.

I turned my back. "We need to speak. Come with me."

We left the dining hall, Bella a few steps behind me. Through the Spiral I led her, down the wide halls and stairs until we were once more deep below, on the sand leading into the hot spring.

Bella put her hands on her hips. "Why here?"

I looked around. "Because everyone would expect you to speak with me in your quarters, or the throne room. If anyone is looking to listen in they will need to come through there." I pointed at the single entrance. "And Peta's going to guard it for us."

Peta grinned up at me, then trotted up the stairs, and plunked herself down in the middle of the doorway.

"Why?"

"Because I am not the only one who is gathering the five stones." I drew a breath. "Raven is hunting them too. I need surprise on my side to get to them faster than him."

I crouched and Bella did the same, her skirt billowing out around her. "Talk to me, Lark. Tell me everything you can."

That much at least she understood. That perhaps there were things I might not be able to share.

"The stones were created by an elemental who could control the wearer." I looked straight at her. "I believe your actions to be at the wishes of this elemental. To fight me, to make it difficult to take the ring." I brushed a hand through the sand.

Bella swallowed hard and slid all the way down to the sand. "That . . . makes a wicked sort of sense. There were things I did that I didn't want to, but when I attacked you . . . I just didn't want you to have the ring. Even though a voice told me to give it up."

My ears all but perked up. "A voice told you to give the ring up?" Perhaps the mother goddess was helping after all.

"Yes, it was faint, but there. Of course, you see how well I listened." She snorted softly.

From the doorway, Peta spoke. "Does this really matter right now?"

She had a point. "Bella, I have to remove the stones from the other three rulers. They have had the stones, and worn them, far longer than you have. The madness that was creeping over you will be even worse with them. And I have to do it before Raven does."

She frowned. "And if you don't?"

"The world will be destroyed. With the five stones, Raven would be strong enough to break our world." Not that I was going to tell them I had the fifth ring safely tucked away. No need to let that particular cat out of the bag.

Her hand went to her throat. "Are you sure?"

"That is what the mother goddess told me," I paused, "but even that is not the whole reason. Ash is not dead,

Bella. I went to his grave. He wasn't in it. The mother goddess will tell me where to find him."

"So you are doing this . . . for yourself? Not to save the world." Her eyes widened, surprise flitting through them.

"I'm doing this for Ash. And it's saving the other families in the process." I bit the words out, fighting the chagrin her implication sparked in me.

"Lark, that isn't like you—"

"You do not know me anymore," I snapped. "I am not the sister who fought for you in the Deep. I am not her. She is dead."

"Then there is only one thing to do." She stood and brushed her skirts off. "I suppose you are flying with your Pegasus to the other rulers since the armbands and the Traveling room do not work."

I stood and nodded. "Yes, I will leave immediately."

"Then I will need to change my clothes." She strode from me. "I will meet you outside the Spiral in an hour."

Oh no, this was not happening. "You aren't coming with me, and even if you were, an hour is too long."

She spun, her eyes flashing. "Am I your queen? Or did you change your vows to serve and obey me when I was handed the throne?"

Lips pressed tightly, I forced myself to nod. "You are my queen."

"Then I will go with you to *visit* my fellow rulers. You need my help, Lark. That much is evident. It will make a good cover for you that you are there to be my Ender as you have been in the past."

I snorted. "I am strong enough."

"It is not your strength I question, sister, but your heart."

Her words were like an arrow piercing my chest. She strode across the sand and up the stairs.

Peta let her go by and then she mewed softly at me, but I barely heard her.

Bella thought she could change the past; that she could draw me out from the dark places I'd receded into. I did not want to hurt her, but I knew disappointment was coming for her if she continued to believe she could save the part of me that was dead and gone.

Moving slowly, I climbed the steps, holding my hands out for Peta. She leapt up to me and curled herself around my neck. "Peta, how can I make her see that it is better to be this way? To be hard and not weak? That weakness is what has brought me to the brink of death time and again. It's what landed me in the oubliette both times. Hesitation."

She purred softly, the sound vibrating along my skin. "It is good to be strong, Lark, to know your weaknesses and conquer them. But to be hard is a dangerous thing; hard can be broken and shattered. Let her come with you. I think it's a good thing to have her at your side."

I made my way up the stairs, lost in my thoughts, so much so that I didn't notice Red until he hovered in front of my face, his feathers brushing against my cheeks.

Startled, I stepped back, my hand going for my spear. The ground shuddered and the Spiral groaned like a wounded animal.

"Peta, go to Bella. Make sure she's safe." Peta bolted up the stairs, shifting into her leopard form between leaps.

Red hovered in front of me, and I held my arm out for him to land. His talons dug into my forearm and I put a hand on his back. His entire body trembled. "What is it?"

"Lark, your father is out of control, the madness has

seized him completely. You have to end this. You are the only one with the training to do it."

Not stop him, but to end this.

I had to be an Ender for the Rim and take my father's life.

bolted through the Spiral. Red launched into the air, leading me out the main doors.

"He's attacking people and no one will stop him. They're afraid because he was the king." The panic in Red's voice was obvious.

"Red, you know—"

"I do. And you must. He wouldn't want this." A tear slipped from the hawk, sparkled in the air and fell to the ground as we ran.

Outside the Spiral was total chaos as I slid to a stop at the edge of the main thoroughfare. Bodies were scattered everywhere and at the foot of the Spiral stood Bella, facing our father, Peta in front of her.

From where I stood I could see the tears stream down her face as she held a hand out to him. He snarled and batted her hand away. Lines of power, deep green and violently aggressive, spiraled up his arms. I was too far away.

The ground erupted under her, sending her flying

backward against the Spiral with a thud that rebounded in the air.

"No!"

He twisted and glared at me. I sprinted toward him, spinning my spear out and around as I ran. Bella's eyes met mine from where she lay, and she nodded. "Do it, Ender Larkspur."

Except I knew it wouldn't be that easy. Basileus hadn't been king based solely on his family line. He was the most powerful Earth Elemental our world had seen.

Until me.

"Peta, I can't engage him with power; we'd destroy the Rim."

"I know."

I looked up. "Red, can you help?" A familiar turning on their charge was not possible, I knew that. So did he.

He dropped to my shoulder and his claws dug in tightly. "Yes. He would not want this, Lark. For all he's done, very little has been within his control." He paused. "Set him free."

Three words and the tears welled in my eyes.

"Peta," I choked on her name, "hamstring him."

Red clung to my shoulder, swaying. He bowed his head, and tucked it against my cheek, his feathers silken. "I bond myself to you, Larkspur."

His words were unexpected in the middle of the chaos and I jerked as a connection formed between us, swift as a rushing wind, the feel of feathers inside my head a strange sensation.

With a cry, he launched into the air and circled us.

Shaking, I spun my spear, and faced my father for what I knew in my heart would be the last time. "Basileus, for the crime of attacking our queen, you are sentenced to death."

If I could get close enough to him, I could put a hand on him. I could stop this before it went any further.

I took a step and the ground softened under me, sucked at my feet. I sidestepped and eyed the distance between us. There was no way I could leap it. There was no way I could do this except to kill him.

His eyes were wild, more white showing than a wild horse running scared. Was he scared? Or—

"Then do it, Ender. Unless you are afraid of an old man?" he snarled.

Perhaps he wasn't as afraid as I'd thought. The lines of power curled around him, deeper and yet brighter than any other time I'd seen him connect to the earth. Wild and out of control. A part of me wondered if that was how the lines looked on me.

I saw his intention. He would rip the Spiral itself apart, destroying what had been created thousands of years ago, unseating Bella in her tenuous hold of the throne.

He gave me no choice and I hardened myself to what I was about to do.

"Peta, now!"

She shot forward, her wicked claws slashing through both his hamstrings, cutting him down and breaking his concentration.

It wasn't enough, though. My father was a powerhouse, legendary in his strength. The ground rumbled and the Spiral shivered as it began to break apart. I hefted my spear. One throw, I wouldn't get another chance like this.

My father flung a hand toward me and the speed of the power was such that I couldn't sidestep him. Vines shot up around me, faster than any lightning bolt as they wrapped around my legs, arms, and neck. I slashed at the vines while they slowly strangled me.

I couldn't think, couldn't even reach for my connection to the earth, the panic was so strong. This was my father. How could this be happening now, when I'd finally forgiven him?

A flash of color, red and tawny brown, caught my eye as Red dove from above, his claws outstretched, a scream erupting from him as he slammed into my father's face. Blood and feathers flew into the air, the sound of flesh tearing blindingly loud in my ears.

Basileus screamed, the vines softened, and I ripped them from me. My father swung his fists at Red, before he grabbed him around the neck. "You stupid bird, I should have roasted you along with the other two."

Good goddess, had he killed Karhu and Hercules?

Red went limp in his hand and I felt his despair as if it were my own. He might have shifted his bond to me, but it was for one reason only.

A familiar would never be able to attack their charge. It was impossible. And so he'd done the only thing he could, and gave himself to someone else. To me.

My father bore down on Red's thin neck, a crack resounding through the air. The bond between Red and me shimmered, and dulled. I ran at them, sliding across the ground to tackle Basileus. I hit him in the midsection, flipped him over backward. Blood from the wounds on his face splattered my arms, the world slowed. Red flopped to the side, boneless.

I slapped a hand against my father's neck, and his pulse slowed under my fingers.

His eyes cleared, and his lips trembled. He looked around him, saw his hawk and let out a strangled cry. He gently lifted Red and cradled him to his chest. "Oh, my friend. My friend, forgive me," he whispered as Red's life faded. I scooped the bird from him with my free hand and lifted him to my face, pressing my cheek against his.

"Red, I can heal you." I offered, already knowing his answer. Because it was the answer Peta would have given.

"No. Let me be free with him. Let us fly together . . . as we were meant to." He closed his eyes and was gone. The bond between us dissipated, and I felt its loss, even though it had only been minutes he'd been mine.

As the feeling of being connected to Red blew away on a whisper of unseen wings, grief roared through me in its wake. I wasn't sure I could do what was being asked of me. I wasn't sure I could end my father's life. He took Red's lifeless body from me and tucked the bird once more to his chest.

"He is right. Let me be free of this madness, Lark. Let me go."

Bella approached from behind, tears streaming down her face. "Lark, is there any other way?"

I stared at my father, wanting the answer to be different. Wanting desperately not to have to make this choice. There was no power in this world that would cure a broken mind, a madness bound up in Spirit and fear, in death and manipulation.

"No. He is right. There is no other way."

Father held his hand out to Bella. "You are the queen our family needs, Belladonna. Do not forget it."

He took her hand and pressed it to his face. "Forgive me for my weakness, daughter."

She fell to her knees and pressed her face against his. "Father."

I closed my eyes, the only privacy I could give them to say their goodbye.

"Lark, do not hesitate," he said. I opened my eyes, the tears making it difficult to see clearly.

"I won't."

"I don't mean only with this, but in your life. Don't hesitate, child. Fear has held you back, the desire to fit in so strong in you, it is blinding. You were never meant to fit in." He brushed a hand along my cheek. "You were meant to burn brighter, to lead the way through the darkness our world faces."

Keeping one hand on his neck, I slipped a dagger from my belt and glanced at Bella. "Are you staying?"

"I will not let you do this alone."

She put her hand over mine as I clenched the dagger. Our people slowly gathered around us, crying softly, tears slipping down cheeks as they saw . . . what? The love of a family destroyed, coming together in the last second. Perhaps.

His eyes closed, and a smile crossed his lips. I thrust the dagger forward, Bella's hand gripped tightly to mine. There was a moment where the image in front of me wavered, and fogged at the edges where I thought perhaps I was dreaming, and I would wake covered in sweat still in my redwood tree house. That the day was a nightmare to be brushed off along with the sleepy dirt in my eyes.

Basileus jerked once, blood bubbled over his lips and his last breath escaped him in a slow exhale that splattered blood on both my face and Bella's. His heart beat once, twice, and then stilled. Jaw ticking, I pulled the dagger free and wiped it on his shirt. "It is done."

Shaking, Bella stood. She spoke to our family, the words white noise in my ears. Something about letting the past go and reaching for the future.

Peta crouched beside me.

I put a hand to the earth and opened it up under him,

burying him right there, at the foot of the Spiral. There were a few murmurs that I stilled with a narrow-eyed glance.

"Bella, if you are coming with me, I'm leaving now." My words were hollow, without inflection. The truth of what I'd had to do sunk in slowly. I'd killed my own father. Even though Bella's hand had been on the dagger, I knew it did not lay on her.

I shook my head. I would not grieve. I would not let it take me into the grave with him.

A red head of hair moved through the crowd, and in seconds Cactus stood in front of me. His nose was still swollen, but his green eyes were soft with emotions I did not want from him. Forgiveness being at the front, love close behind it, compassion somewhere in the mix.

Peta tugged at my leg. "He could help in the Pit. You know that."

Damn, she was right.

"Lark, I'm sorry about . . ." He didn't seem to know how to say he was sorry I had to kill my own father. Not like that was something he could find on a Hallmark card.

I held a hand up. "Don't. There is nothing you can say to make this better. But you can help me."

His eyes brightened. "Anything. You know I'd do anything for you."

I swallowed back the words that almost came out. Like why don't you do as I ask and leave me alone? "I need you to go to the Pit. See what the atmosphere is like, and see if you can get close to Fiametta. See if you get any glimpse of Blackbird."

He frowned, and slowly nodded. "I can do that. Are you going to tell me why?"

I didn't need the tightening of Peta's claws on my lower leg to keep my mouth shut. "No, I can't."

Peta chimed in. "Business of the mother goddess."

"Oh. When will you be there?" He took a step toward me, and I glared at him, stopping him.

I shook my head and winced at the aches and bruises from the near-strangulation I'd endured. "I'm not sure. Soon, though. You'll have to find a way there. The armbands aren't working."

"I'll take a plane," he said. "I've done that before." His words surprised me. It was easy for me to forget there was an entire human world out there. And that Cactus had no problem interacting with it.

"That's good."

Worm shit, our conversation wouldn't have been more stilted if the words themselves had been frozen. I turned my back on him.

"Shazer!" I called out.

"I am here." He trotted toward me from between the Ender Barracks and the Spiral. "Where do we fly first?"

"The Deep." I hoped that it would be easier to deal with Finley. *Hope* being the relative word. With a long-standing friendship, there was plenty of reason for me to visit her, and for her to let me draw close. Bella's daughter River had ties to the Deep as well, which was another reason.

Bella touched my arm. "I am ready."

Damn. I was hoping she would stay behind to grieve properly. "Let's go then."

Shazer went to one knee. "Your Majesty."

Bella hurried to his side and mounted, her pale green skirts bunching up but still managing to cover most of her leg, though I noticed Shazer looking. I lifted my hands to him and he winked.

"She has nice legs, don't blame me for looking."

Once a male, always a male, apparently.

Bella stared out over the crowd from Shazer's back. "In my absence, Niah and River will oversee the running of the Rim. Look to them, and know I am going on the business of the mother goddess, to do her will, to keep the Rim, and our world, safe." Apparently she'd overheard Peta's words. If nothing else, the crowd murmured and nodded at her declaration.

What surprised me though was who she left in charge. Seemed I wasn't the only one who the announcement shocked. Niah was at the back of the crowd, tears still running down her face even as her eyes widened and she shook her head. Bella nodded at her. "Yes, Niah. You."

"Good luck, Niah." I lifted a hand to her, and she raised one in return.

"Be careful, Lark. Things are not as they seem, not even now."

I shrugged. "They never have been, old one."

I leapt up behind Bella, Peta right behind me. She put herself between Bella and me, curling up in the puff of Bella's voluminous skirts.

No words were cast between us as Shazer galloped across the Rim, gaining speed before he leapt into the air, his wings driving hard to lift us all.

I reached forward and put my arms around my sister. She clutched my arms to her as the sobs broke through, her body shaking with the force of them.

"Lark, we killed him. I know we had to, but I—"

"No, this is not on you, Bella. It was my dagger, and I did it."

I leaned my head forward and pressed it to her back, no cries escaping me. No other words I could give would comfort her. The truth was we'd had to do it, and she knew that.

Maybe Peta was right, maybe I was too hard.

Then again, I was about to go up against three elemental rulers in their places of power while madness rode them.

Weakness was not something I could afford.

CHAPTER 9

e only flew a few hours before night fell, and Shazer landed at the edge of a cleared field. "With a quick break, I could fly through the rest of the night without another stop."

"No, Bella needs to sleep. We'll stop for the night," I said, dismounting and then holding a hand out to my sister. She took it and slid from his back with a wince but she shook her head. "No, I think we should keep going. I'm fine. A short break will be enough." She paused and rubbed at her backside. "It's been a long time since I've been horseback riding."

Shazer snorted. "Pegasus riding."

She blinked up at him and smiled. "Right, Pegasus."

Above us, the night sky twinkled, black and splattered with stars. I looked at Bella. She still had our father's blood on one cheek. I motioned with my head for her to follow me. The sound of a creek drew me.

Beside me, Peta eyed the fireflies that flickered here and there. I rolled my eyes. "Go for it. I won't tell anyone."

With a funny mew she leapt into the air, batting at the bugs. They were almost as fast as her, though, and darted away as she pounced and chased. I smiled and looked up. Bella watched me, a smile on her lips, too.

"She's like a kitten still."

"Sometimes. Other times she seems the oldest soul I know." I pushed through the long grass and down a small embankment to a shallow stream. I stepped into the creek and sunk to my knees before splashing my face and arms. Pink swirls of dried blood washed away in the shimmers of dark water that shone in the bright moonlight, curling through the current and then gone as if they never were.

Bella stepped into the water beside me, her skirt caught up with one hand. I took the edges of the material and held it for her as she cleaned her face and arms. In silence we stepped out onto the embankment and headed to where Peta lay crouched in the long grass. She'd shifted into her leopard form.

I gave a short laugh. "You think you can catch the bugs when you're bigger?"

Her ear flicked at me but otherwise she didn't move. In an explosion of speed, she shot twenty feet into the air to snag a bug, slamming it with both paws.

Bella burst out laughing and I joined in. "Damn, reflexes like a cat."

Peta turned and faced us, lifting her lips so we could see her teeth.

And the glowing firefly in her mouth, lighting her up like a human's Halloween pumpkin.

I choked on the laughter, unable to believe that she hadn't squashed the bug completely. She opened her mouth and the firefly flew out, bobbled once, and rose into the air. Peta licked her lips. "Bet you two can't catch one."

"Challenge accepted!" Bella laughed and ran into the long grass. I stood and stared.

"We're on a deadline, Bella. I can't be playing—"

Shazer butted me from behind. "Go play."

Peta nodded. "Go play."

Bella stood in the middle of the fireflies as she spun and looked at me. "Afraid you'll lose?"

I took my spear from my back and slowly swirled it in front of me. Through the bond to Peta, fear and sadness rolled. I drove the spear into the ground, haft first. "You are going to be sorry you said that."

The tension in the air heightened and I let go of the spear and ran into the long grass after Bella. She spun and ran from me, and the tension was broken as we did our best to grab the fireflies from their nightly dance.

Screeching and laughing, we raced after the tiny bugs as though we were children and not full-grown adults. Peta dodged between us, knocking us down more than once, often right as we got close to capturing our intended prey.

A flash of white streaked by, Shazer with his neck outstretched as he snapped his teeth at a firefly that struggled to stay out of reach.

Bella gasped for breath and clutched at her sides. I stood next to her, breathing hard, not sure exactly why I was playing when I should have been off saving the world. Stopping Blackbird from getting the stones first.

"Because if you have nothing to fight for, saving the world doesn't mean much, does it?" Peta sat on top of my feet, warming them. She looked up at me. "The world, and all it is, has to mean something to you again, Lark. You helped the Tracker save the world from the demons. But that wasn't really you. You did it because you had to. This time, it's your choice."

"Mind-reading cat," I muttered.

"What do you expect? I'm special." She grinned up at me.

I waved a hand to catch Shazer's attention. "We need to go."

He trotted over and put his nose against my chest. "I hate to say the pussy is right, but she is." He blew out a hot gust from his nose, warming my skin as Peta warmed my feet. She took a swat at him.

"Don't be vulgar."

"I'm not."

"You are too, and you know it." She frowned up at him.

He shrugged and went to one knee as Bella approached. Flushed from running about, she mounted with ease. "I think Peony was right, I need to stop trying to fit into the same size as when I was sixteen."

I snorted as Peta and I leapt up behind her, Peta once more worming her way between us. "I'm glad you don't try that when you are in your leopard form."

"Me too. You're not all fluff, you know," Shazer bit out as he galloped across the field.

Bella crunched forward and slapped his neck. "It's not polite to talk about a lady's weight."

He grunted as he leapt into the air. "When you start being a beast of burden, you get to say whatever you like about the size of people's asses."

She gasped, Peta let out a growl, and I rolled my eyes. "No comment about my weight?"

"Goddess, no, you'd probably cut my wings off."

There was a moment of uncomfortable silence and then I laughed softly. "True enough, I might."

"You wouldn't." Bella twisted to look at me, her hair swirling out around her. I shrugged.

"Well, not on your behalf, I wouldn't. I saw you naked earlier, remember? No hiding your ass from me."

Her jaw dropped and horror flickered through her eyes. "Am I that fat?"

"Goddess, no, I was teasing!" I leaned forward and patted her on the head as though she were the younger sibling and not me. "You don't look any different to me than you did when I was a child, Bella. Still the big sister I want to be when I grow up."

Tears filled her eyes and she blinked them away. "That's the nicest thing you could have said."

"Well, I'm nothing if not full of sugar and spice."

Peta snorted. "Heavy on the spice, I think."

Shazer snorted. "Are you three going to have this hen party the entire time? My ears are on the verge of bleeding."

"Yes," the three of us answered in unison. Peta purred softly between us.

"This is how it is meant to be."

I knew what she meant, but it scared me. I wrapped my arms around Bella again and we clung to each other like children fending off the night together. I only hoped that was not what reality turned out to be.

We flew through the night, and early the next morning we were over the southeastern seaboard. The Deep lay in the section of the ocean the humans nicknamed the Bermuda Triangle.

The water was brilliantly blue below us, and I could see

a good distance into it. Triangular fins popped up here and there. Bella shuddered. I held tighter to her. Neither of us had the greatest memories from our time in the Deep.

"You were there, after River was born?" I asked.

"Yes." Just one word, but that was all that was needed. She'd done it to keep her daughter safe from her psychotic mother, Cassava.

The sun had climbed only a few degrees when we dipped through the sky toward the white beach of the Deep.

Shazer landed lightly, with only a single hop, on the beach at the eastern edge. The sand was so white, it almost glowed. The spires of the main holdings rose into the bright sunlight, glinting as though they'd been shined just this morning.

"We need to make this happen as fast as we can, once we do it," I said, finally speaking out loud the plan that had formed as we'd flown. "There are ambassadors here from every family. There were none in the Rim. Once we take the stone from Finley, the other ambassadors will have time to get ahead of us and warn Fiametta and Samara."

"Only if it goes badly." Bella smoothed out her skirts and I stared at her until she lifted her eyes. "What?"

"*If* it goes badly? I think we need to count on that."

I started across the sand, heading for a paved section. Bella remained where she was. I turned. "What?"

"I just . . . I have not been here since you were banished. Finley and I were close then, but those are not the memories that bother me."

Of course not. The first time in the Deep together, I was her Ender. She was an ambassador. Things had not gone well then, either. Not for her, at least.

I went to her side. "Do you want to leave?"

She shook her head. "No. I only needed a moment to gather myself."

I waited, feeling the need to move grow until I almost grabbed her. A figure at the edge of the sand approached and raised a hand to us.

"Your Majesty, we had no word of you coming." Dolph, my one-time teacher and fellow Ender, strode toward us. I took a step back, allowing Bella to lead. She nodded to Dolph, her face smoothing over in a perfect mask.

"Ender Dolph, thank you. It is of great importance that I speak with your queen. A new threat comes at our families."

He frowned. "We have heard nothing."

"I know, that is why I came in person rather than send a messenger." She strode toward him, and I kept step in time with her.

"Finley is not here at the moment," Dolph said. "But you are welcome to wait for her. I will have rooms ready for you."

Bella nodded. "That will be fine."

He led us through the Deep, toward the spire that rested nearest the center. Shazer veered off as we drew close. "I smell . . . uh . . . oats. I will be in the stable if you need me."

I patted his side and he trotted off down the cobblestone street, wings bobbing.

"I do not smell any oats," Peta grumped. "But I do smell a mare in heat."

I clamped my lips shut tightly so as not to laugh. This was not a time for laughter; this was a time for focus.

Once more, I stepped into the Deep, the feeling of being out of my element—literally—surrounding me. The halls were not much changed from my previous visits. Sandstone walls embedded with seashells and pearls, the odd starfish here and there. Smooth stone under our feet, the constant sound of water trickling somewhere. There were not many Undines about, but those that were smiled when they saw us. Behind the smiles I saw suspicion and distrust.

But maybe that was just me.

The room Dolph took us to was not the one we'd stayed in before, though it might as well have been as the décor was the same. It felt like we'd stepped back in time.

Not something I wanted to do.

As soon as the door shut, Bella flopped onto the bed. "I could sleep for days. I'm exhausted."

I lay beside her. "Might as well. We have to wait on Finley anyway."

We were quiet for only a moment before Bella rolled to face me. "Do you love Cactus?"

I groaned. "Please, I do not want to—"

"Come on. Tell me." She pushed me lightly with one hand. I drew in a deep breath but didn't face her.

"I did once, before . . . before the oubliettes. I think I could have settled down with him."

"And now?"

I scrunched my shoulders up. "He is not the one for me. Peta has known it all along, and I know it too. Now."

"But he loves you."

I grunted.

Bella leaned forward. "And you're using that love. Lark, that is awful."

Anger overcame fatigue and I sat up. "Listen. I've flat out told him off. He doesn't want to listen. That's not my fault. Surely you have suitors who won't listen to you?"

Her lips parted. "Of course not."

The lie was as thick as pudding in the air between us. "Spill it. Who is chasing you?"

"No one."

I snorted. "Come on."

Her lips twitched. "Maybe one or two."

"And of course you told them off?"

Her eyes widened. "One is Fiametta's son, so no, I have not told him off."

Time for my eyes to widen. "A true merge of two families? Oooh, the drama."

"I never said I was even going to—"

"Please, you don't have to marry him to carry his child." I lay back on the bed, instantly regretting my words. "Bella, I'm sorry, I didn't mean . . ."

"Lark, don't. Requiem was a long time ago, and I was a fool. I thought I was strong enough to face him on my own." She sighed and lay beside me. "And as much of a monster as he was, he gave me the most amazing daughter."

I wanted to reach over and take her hand, or hug her. But I couldn't make myself move. I wasn't sure I could ever be so forgiving of Requiem. Or the other monsters I'd faced.

"Go to sleep, Lark," she said as though she were in charge.

I closed my eyes, knowing I should have been bothered by the fact that I did as she asked without question; old habits dying hard. Still, I fell asleep within seconds.

My mind, though, did not allow me any respite, as dreams haunted my rest. They battled for my attention, swinging from the war we'd fought against Orion and the demons, to the mother goddess laughing at me, to Blackbird trying to bed me as I lay tied down and unable to fight.

A violent shiver woke me at one point. The breeze

coming in from the wide window cooled the sweat along my bare skin. I groped for a blanket and someone placed a thick duvet over me. Peta crept up in her snow leopard form, stretching out alongside my body, and sharing her warmth with me.

Bella dropped an arm around my waist. "Just dreams, Lark. They are just dreams. Let them go."

Again, I obeyed her, and relaxed once more.

The fear left, the pain of all I'd lost slipped away. I fell asleep again, this time safe in knowing, if nothing else, I had my sister with me.

More the fool was I for believing my life would come together so smoothly.

CHAPTER 10

T he banging on the door jerked me out of a dead sleep. I scrambled out of bed, my spear in my hand even as I reached for the power of the earth before my eyes were even fully open.

Spirit and Earth rumbled through me, dangerous in their current state of unpredictability.

"Easy, Lark. We are not surrounded by enemies," Peta soothed.

I shook myself, and quickly let go of my connection to the earth but not my spear.

I strode to the door and opened it with a jerk. In front of me was a petite woman, in all white, one of the Undine slaves. Usually they were human, captured when they ventured too close to the Deep.

She lifted clear blue eyes to me. Elemental power swirled along the edges of her arms as she tapped into the water around us. Obviously not a human, but worse was what I saw in her intention. The lines all but spelled out what she was going to do. Something so simple, and so effective, that no one would realize what had happened to me.

The slave was going to fill my lungs with water so I died without a sound, drowned on dry land.

I grabbed her around the throat and lifted her straight up so her feet dangled. "Not quick enough, assassin."

Her eyes bulged, the color on her arms flared, and I clamped my mouth shut. I bore down until I felt her pulse slow under my fingers, frantic and then pausing between each beat. Her eyes rolled into the back of her head and the lines of blue power faded from her arms. Only when I was sure she was out cold did I let go, letting her drop to the floor with a meaty thump.

"Lark, what is going on?" Bella ran across to me, her hair and skirts seriously rumpled, yet she still looked like a queen.

"Bella, stay here. I don't want you in the middle of this."

She put a hand on my arm, slowing me. "Lark, I am here to help you. What happened?"

My jaw ticked twice before I answered. "She tried to kill me."

Peta sniffed the assassin at my feet. "Half-breed, I think, which explains the slave whites."

My anger grew in leaps and bounds. "Well, Bella, time to see if you can smooth this over, then. Time to be a diplomat before I kill someone."

Bella let out a sigh, but followed me into the hall. She swept her hands over her skirts several times, knocking the worst of the wrinkles out, then swiftly pulled her hair into a loose braid. "I wish you would give me time to properly clean up."

"No time, you know that. If I have an assassin on me,

for all we know . . ." I paused and changed what I was going to say at the last second, "that which we seek has already been snagged by Blackbird."

"You have to be wrong," she murmured.

I hoped I was, but an assassin coming after me was no small thing. There was no way Finley would allow it.

Dragging the would-be assassin behind, I stalked toward the throne room.

"You know this isn't Finley's doing," Peta said, her voice rather carefully neutral.

"Why do you say it like that? You think I'm going in there and accusing her of trying to kill me?"

"I hope not," Bella said.

I stopped and stared at her. "I may be a bad-ass bitch, but I'm not crazy."

Bella's lips twitched. "You're hardly the bitch you think you are. Bad ass, absolutely."

Peta laughed, though it was under her breath.

At the throne room doors, I didn't pause, just pushed my way through. The woman I dragged behind me groaned as she came around.

I threw her forward. Her body rolled across the ground, flipping and flopping like a fish out of water until she stopped at the base of Finley's throne.

The queen of the Deep lifted a dark blue eyebrow. She'd grown up since I'd first met her, both in body and mind. Her blue hair had deepened in color to a near violet and was swept up in a twist that left the lines of her face bare, making her seem older than she really was.

But it was her eyes I watched closely. Her blue eyes held her secrets close and I couldn't read her, or what she thought about our sudden appearance. To be fair, she'd fooled me even when she'd been a child, so it shouldn't have surprised me that as an adult she was even better at keeping her face a mask of neutral emotions.

"Lark, I trust you have found something to your displeasure?"

"Do you know this woman?" I tipped my chin in the direction of the slave at her feet.

Finley shook her head, without ever looking down. "No. Should I?"

"She tried to kill me."

From the edges of the room, Finley's Enders shifted, appearing to materialize out of thin air. The slave woman groaned again and pushed herself to her knees. "I am a lowly servant. I did nothing, Your Majesty, but bring her towels."

Finley rose and walked down the few steps so she stood on the floor with me. She tipped her head to one side. "Slave, why would Lark attack you?"

The woman stirred and went to her knees, folding herself in half. "She's crazy. We all know that. The Destroyer. She is here to hurt us as she hurt the Eyrie."

I snorted and smiled at Finley. "If she was bringing us towels, she forgot them, since nothing was in her hands." What a crock of horseshit.

Finley did not smile back. Peta tightened her grip on my shirt. "This is not good, Lark."

Bella stepped forward. "Your Majesty, I was there. This woman attacked my sister, the heir to the Rim's throne, without provocation."

I went stock-still. That was news to me, and not welcome news at that. I'd already turned the throne down once. I would do it again if Bella tried to push it on me. But that was a problem for another time.

The Enders around us shifted again, tightening the circle.

"Queen Belladonna," Finley said, "I believe you would say anything to protect your family."

Her implication was clear: she thought Bella was lying for me. This was going downhill faster than an avalanche in the spring melt.

I held my hands up over my head, facing the palms to Finley. "I have never harmed you, Finley. I've done nothing but be your friend in all the years we have known one another."

"You destroyed the Eyrie, Lark. Do not think anyone has forgotten that, no matter that it happened many years ago," she said. "You could sink the Deep, if you chose to."

Her words were not the words of the queen I knew. Damn it to hell and back. The sapphire had to be affecting her, and whoever controlled her through it. From the third finger on her left hand it glinted, as if winking at me. "Finley—"

"*Queen* Finley," she said, her eyes hardening ever so slightly. "You may stay another night if you wish and feel the need to rest. You and your sister are our guests. But that only goes so far for one as volatile as you. And I make this concession only because of what you have done for me in the past, and because your queen is here to look after you and keep you on a short tether." As though I were a way-ward child.

I gave her a stiff bow, knowing that getting the stone from her was going to be far harder than I'd hoped. Maybe I would have to use the fake sapphire after all. "We will be gone by sunrise tomorrow."

Finley didn't incline her head; she snapped her fingers

and an Ender stepped forward. His face reminded me of a boy I'd known once. Sting, and his twin sister Ray, had helped me in my battle to defeat Requiem. And here he stood before me, an Ender. His eyes glittered with the same cheeky humor I'd seen in him as a child. He dared to give me a wink, and I shook my head ever so slightly.

Finley snapped her fingers again. "Ender Sting, take the slave to the healer. Make sure she is not injured badly and can still attend to her duties."

"As you command, my Queen." He bowed at the waist, then bent and scooped up the slave.

He past close enough by me to whisper, "Ray is in the library. She will want to see you."

Again, I nodded ever so slightly. No need to piss off Finley more by fraternizing with her Enders.

Bella laid a hand on my arm, ever so lightly, pressuring me to step back as she moved forward.

"Your Majesty, if I may speak to you? There are matters concerning the four families that warrant our attention. There are wars being waged in the human world we must take notice of as I believe they will soon be at our doorsteps. It is not something we can bury our heads against."

Finley's eyes grew thoughtful. "Of course, but the Destroyer is not welcome to our conversation."

Bella nodded. "You are dismissed, Ender Larkspur."

I knew this game all too well; we'd played it before. I gave another stiff bow. "As you wish." With a quick spin, I strode from the women.

Once outside the throne room, and halfway to our quarters, I finally spoke. "Peta, tell me you remember Finley was not like that before, that it is not just me seeing this change in her."

"She was not like this. Something has happened, of that

much I agree. It would seem the mother goddess was correct about the stones. Finley is even more distrusting than Bella." Peta shook her head. "Of course, she has had the ring in her possession almost as long as Bella, and if Finley's behavior is any indicator, she uses it more."

"So now we wait for a chance," I breathed. Waiting was something I could do, but I didn't like it. Not when I knew the longer we waited, the more chance that Blackbird would beat us to the other rulers. Damn it.

Sting said his sister was in the library, but I needed more than a quiet place to wait. I needed to move, to feel my blood pumping. In movement I found my peace, and maybe I'd even find a solution to how to get the stone from Finley.

Every family had a place that was my home away from home. Even here in the Deep.

The Enders Barracks.

I stopped at a doorway leading outside the palace and into the main courtyards of the Deep. Fountains splashed, the sound of water beckoning me out, but it wasn't the water I headed to. Across a small rope bridge was the Enders Barracks, and while it wasn't my barracks, it would do for a substitute.

I hurried across the swaying bridge while Peta clung to me. No point in looking down. I knew what was below the unstable rope bridge. Lots and lots of water, just waiting to swallow me. I shivered and kept my eyes locked on the far side, doing my best not to recall memories I'd much rather forget.

I stepped off the rope bridge and onto the solid footing of the barracks with a quiet sigh.

A twang wrapped through my chest, thinking of the girl who ruled the Deep. I'd saved Finley, helped her gain her throne, and thought she'd been someone I could turn to . . . she'd even fought for me at the battle against the demons. It was as if the second I was set on this quest, the rulers knew I was coming for them. That wasn't possible, was it?

Yet . . . maybe it was. The mother goddess said the stones could be used to control those who wore them. And Shazer had said his creator was still alive . . . worm shit and goblin piss, who was it?

Peta leapt from my shoulder and shifted as she landed. "Perhaps Bella can get the stone from Finley."

"Perhaps." I doubted it, though. Finley's eyes had said it all; she did not trust me. And because of me, she would not trust Bella either. "I only hope Bella doesn't try and take it from her."

"Goddess, that could go badly."

"You think?" I snorted.

"Bella is smarter than that. She knows when to attack and when to retreat and feign defeat."

I walked beside Peta, a hand on her back as we entered the training room for the Deep's Enders.

I went to the center of the room and swung my spear lazily from its holder, thinking about all the possibilities in front of me. All the questions I had no answer to.

I whipped the spear up and over my head, spinning it as hard as I could.

Circling, I let the movement of the weapon take me where it would as Peta sat and watched.

I swept through the forms as if there were an opponent in front of me, my spear slicing through the air soundlessly and deadly, sweat slowly popping out on my arms and face as I quickened the movements.

Whirling the spear through the air, I shadow-fought

with opponents only I could see until the sweat rolled over my entire body, slicking me from head to foot. I lost track of time as I fell into the rhythm I'd perfected in all my years in the desert.

"Mind if I join you, Larkspur?" A deep voice startled me out of my thoughts. I spun around, spear at the ready. A man leaned against the edge of the doorway and I took him in with a single sweep of my eyes. I'd seen him only days before; there was no way I'd mistake him, though there were changes in his appearance.

The man from the graveyard.

Closer up, I could see details I'd not noted before.

He was taller than me, and his build was well muscled and looked as though he was used to fighting, if the scars on his forearms and the puckered scar that ran across his collarbone were any indication. Dark blue eyes surrounded by a rim of gold stared at me as if weighing my worth. He ran a hand over his head, scrubbing at his short dark brown hair. The color of chocolate was my first thought. He'd cut the long ponytail off, but it didn't fool me.

With those eyes, he could be a shape shifter.

I shook my head.

"The floor is yours, if you tell me why you are following me."

He smiled and white teeth flashed. "Ah, it is so seldom I have the chance to spar with someone who favors my own weapon." He tugged a spear from his side, snapping the two pieces together before swirling it in front of him. The make was identical to my own, down to the leather-wrapped handle.

I frowned. I'd never seen a spear that broke down like mine before.

I glanced at Peta who nodded, her green eyes soft as though she'd only just woken up. "You can always use the practice."

"He's the one from the graveyard. You think it's safe?" I spoke loud enough that I knew he would hear me.

She didn't answer me, just trotted away without a backward glance. My adrenaline spiked and I tightened my grip on my weapon. What the hell?

"Peta?"

"She's off to check on something. So you and I can talk, Lark." He swung the spear so that it resembled my own, in a lazy wide circle.

I stepped back and beckoned him forward with a hand. He stepped toward me, a smile on his lips, and something in the air shifted.

I brought my own weapon up and settled into a crouch. I'd seen him do nothing, pull on no lines of power, and yet I felt it along my skin. He was using his ability with Spirit. I gritted my teeth. I would not be manipulated again.

"I am at a disadvantage. You know my name, but I do not know yours."

He chuckled and settled into a fighting stance across from me. "No? Can you not guess? I have been watching you for a long time, Lark. I knew your mother. Trained her actually." He stepped forward, his spear shooting at me in a fast thrust. I blocked him, spinning sideways in a full circle so I brought my blade back to waver between us.

"It appears you like your weapon far better than she did; that will save you one day, I think." He smiled, and there wasn't a mean thing about it. And yet I couldn't help but be disturbed.

"My mother wasn't trained to fight." I swept the blade

down toward his left knee. He jumped straight up, bringing his spear crashing to the ground, pinning the haft of mine.

I stumbled back, pulling a knife from my side. Ender rule 101. Never leave home with less than two weapons.

"She was trained to fight, even if she chose not to. She didn't understand Spirit. Nor how it truly worked. It was her downfall." He frowned. "I am hoping you will not make the same mistake as her."

Spirit. What would he know of Spirit, unless . . . my jaw dropped as I stared at him. "Talan?"

He bowed at the waist, making a huge sweep with his arms and spear. "The one and only."

Mother goddess have mercy, he couldn't be. But then . . . it made a wicked sort of sense, except for one thing.

"What . . . why did you send Peta away, then?"

"Because she would not understand why I am here. And I am not ready to fully face the fact she loves you more than she ever loved me." His eyes shuttered to half-mast and he gave me a small smile.

"Because you let her believe you died." I spat the words at him, anger on her behalf snapping through me.

"Easy, Lark. There is much you don't understand. I show myself to you so you know you are not alone." He twisted his spear, breaking it down, and hung it from his waist. Tucking a foot under my spear, he flipped it toward me. I caught it, but did not break it down.

"Not alone? I have Peta." And Bella. And Ash when I found him.

"She cannot teach you all you need to know when it comes to Spirit." He shrugged. "She'll keep you alive, though, and that is all you need right now. To survive a little longer."

My jaw twitched. "So you thought you'd come by, introduce yourself, and then leave? Some help."

His lips twitched. "Your time with me is not yet here, Lark—"

"Are you insane?" If I could have frowned harder, I'm sure my face would have split in half. "My time with you? You show up to taunt me, then to offer me help only to take it away—"

"I am the only one who can train you. Even now Spirit has begun to wreak havoc on your control. So I will tell you this, to prove I mean you no harm. Your power is out of balance because *you* are out of balance. Find your center, and Spirit will ease off. We can go from there when your training begins." There was softness in his eyes, almost like he cared. Like for some reason my mental state truly mattered to him.

I took a step back, wanting to believe it would be that easy. "Why?"

Why for so many reasons.

Talan held a hand out to me. "The world is a far bigger place than any of the families realize, and you and I are nearly the last of ours. I have to try and teach you."

"I see your training kept my mother alive." Anger and fear making my words hard.

He didn't flinch. "She made her choice, Lark. As you will make yours. Right now, you are rootbound, and your past holds you so tightly, you cannot grow into the power you are meant to be. You will be forced to make a decision soon, though. One that will change your life forever. Either you will remain as you are, tangled in the past, or you will reach for the future with both hands." He drew in a long breath. "I will find you when the time draws close. And if you want to come with me before then . . ." He flipped something at me. I let the object drop to my feet, never taking my eyes from him.

Talan stood there, watching me watch him. "Your time to take the stones from the elemental leaders is coming to a close, that much is true."

A chill swept through me. "How did you know?"

He didn't directly answer me. "They are far more addictive in their power than even you understand. Your sister rarely wore hers, and you saw how she fought you. You, someone she loves dearly, she would have killed you. You did them all a disservice giving them the stones in the first place."

My jaw dropped. "It's not like they came with an instruction manual. And the battle against Orion and his demons would never have been won without that extra strength."

I felt as though I was in a battle of my own, one where I was rapidly losing ground. He was wrong. We'd needed that strength.

He shook his head, his eyes incredibly sad. "More people would have died, yes, that is true. But the battle itself did not weigh on your shoulders, Larkspur. It weighed on the Tracker and her heart. Your pride made you believe you were integral to a battle that had nothing to do with you. Your battle is yet to come."

His words cut through me, like a spear thrown by a giant, piercing me through my chest. "What are you saying?"

"The battle would have been won without you, Lark. You think too highly of yourself, and it will be your downfall. Pride . . . you have seen how it destroys leaders. And whether you like it or not, Destroyer, you are a leader of a sort."

He took a step back, then another, while I fought with my emotions.

Humiliation, heartsick, physically sick. I went to my knees and gagged, unable to stop my body's reaction to his words. What if he was right? What if I should not have been at that battle?

My whole body shook as his words circled me like vultures waiting for me to lie back and let them pick me apart. I gripped the haft of my spear, as if that would ground me.

I closed my eyes and replayed the battle in my head, seeing it piece by piece, the steps we'd taken to survive, so that more would survive than would die.

So not all hope was lost.

"No, he's wrong. The help was needed." But was I? Or was I fooling myself so I didn't see he was right? That I was too full of pride to realize the damage I'd done?

I couldn't shake the possibility he could be right.

With my eyes squeezed shut tight, I stayed where I was, fighting the emotions that would turn me into an indecisive mess. I jerked, my spine snapping straight. I would not be turned into a weak, fearful girl again.

Never again.

My father's final words soothed me. Do not hesitate.

I opened my eyes, and of course, Talan was gone. I scooped up the object he'd tossed to me, as Peta padded back in. "I didn't see anyone out there. Did you hear something? Is that why you sent me outside?"

My heart clenched. He'd played with her mind, and I knew if I questioned her now it would only make me look crazy. Damn him.

"I thought I did." I hurried to the door, visually sweeping the area. There was no sign of Talan, no sign he'd ever been there. Damn. "I guess I was hearing things."

Her eyes filled with concern and I glanced at the object in my hand. A thick bracelet made of a clear, foggy material.

I rubbed my fingers over it, knowing the sensation the second I did it. I flung the plastic bracelet across the room, bouncing it off the far wall. Fear and horror sliced through my gut. The bracelet was made of the same material as the oubliettes that had held me for so many years.

Talan had given me a piece of my prison to wear.

"I'll be damned before I ever put that on." I didn't care that Peta looked at me like I was losing my mind.

"What is it?"

I closed my eyes and took in deep, long breaths as I fought to calm my heart. I had to be smart about this, I needed to be realistic no matter how difficult it was. No matter how much I might hate Talan for his words, for the doubt he set to spout in me and the fear the bracelet raised.

Though it took everything I had to make my feet move in the direction of the bracelet, I walked across the room. With a swift movement, I bent and scooped it up a second time, sliding it into the leather bag at my side. "It's a tool, and one I hate," I said, "but I am not the child who throws a tantrum and cuts her nose off to spite her face. There is a chance I might need it at some point."

Peta's eyebrows rose, as did the fear in her. I held a hand out to her. "I know it doesn't make sense."

"It's a piece of plastic," Peta said. "How can it possibly help you?"

I tightened the loop on my leather bag so the bracelet was no longer visible. Even so, I couldn't help the shudder that rippled through me. "I will explain . . . later."

Her shoulders drooped and true sorrow passed through the bond between us. I went to my knees and held my arms out wide. She rushed into me, knocking me off balance.

"Please trust me, Peta. Please." Talan obviously didn't want her to know he'd contacted me, and while I didn't completely trust him, for now I had to agree with him on that. I didn't want Peta to know he was around either.

Mostly because a part of me feared he was wrong and that she loved him best and always would.

That she would leave me to be his familiar again.

"It is not you I don't trust, but the things that have been done to you. The things you've faced without me at your side to buffer them," she said.

I closed my eyes, burying my face in her fur. "I know, Peta. I know."

stood and disentangled Peta from me. The past was of no consequence to me now, I had to believe that, or I would drive myself mad with wondering if I could have done things differently. Or wondering if I should never have interfered at all.

She looked up at me, her green eyes thoughtful. "So now what? We wait on Bella to work her magic?"

I doubted it would be as easy as all that. "You were here, during my banishment?"

"Yes, I searched the libraries of all the families as you asked. Learned everything I could and then some. The Deep holds the oldest records of all the families and I learned much here." Her eyes went thoughtful. "Why?"

"What my father said, about the old elemental and the connection to the mother goddess. Do you think that was his madness, or did you ever come across something like that in your studies?"

Her eyes narrowed. "What are you thinking? I can almost feel your mind working."

I shrugged. "What he said has stayed with me, which makes me think there is truth in it somewhere. What if the story was not about the mother goddess, but an elemental that had been powerful like her? And what if that elemental was still alive, and causing grief, controlling the rulers? Shazer said an elemental made him and the stones. Could there be some connection between them? A story that has been twisted from its original meaning, but the center of it still truth?"

Peta tipped her head back and twitched the tip of one rounded ear. "Maybe. But how would you find out?"

"You said the Deep had the oldest records. If there was info about that elemental, this is where it would be, wouldn't it?"

Excitement zipped from Peta through the bond to me. "Yes, the Undines have an excellent section of old bits and pieces, old papers that have no true connection to anything but that they keep because of their age."

And Ray would be in the library. Perhaps she would be able to help me yet again in my search for truth.

Peta bounded ahead of me, through the door and across the rope bridge, with the nimbleness only a cat had, before I'd even stepped foot on the swaying structure. "Slow down."

"Hurry up," she called over her shoulder. "You need to find a way to improve speed and reflexes. Cat-like, that's what you need!"

I shook my head, but let the smile drift across my lips.

The tip of her tail twitched as she waited for me. Again, I hurried over the bridge, not looking down, only ahead. The smell of the Deep swirled around me: salt water, seaweed, a faint hint of tropical fruits, and sun-heated sand. I stepped off the far side of the bridge. "You see my eyes? Not violet. No shape shifting in my future."

"True." She bobbed her head. "Then again, it's not like you've followed the rules so far. Why not try?"

Laughing, I shook my head but said nothing to dispute her. We both knew it wasn't possible.

We crossed the white sand, and before long, stepped onto the cobblestone streets. We approached the stables and I slowed. Set up like an open barn with no real stalls, the stable was heavily bedded with dried seaweed for the live-stock. Shazer dozed under the shelter off to one side. His head jerked up as I approached, his nostrils flaring.

"We leaving?"

"Tomorrow morning." I paused in front of him. "Your creator, did he have a name?"

He ruffled his wings and stretched out his front legs. "I don't even remember my own name, and you expect me to remember the name of the elemental who made me?"

"Couldn't hurt to ask. Seeing as how we may have to deal with him at some point."

Both Shazer and Peta stared at me with open mouths.

"What?" Peta blurted.

Shazer spluttered. "I hope you're kidding. Tell me you are joking, Lark."

The words had slipped out, but as soon as they'd escaped me I wished I'd caught them. Not because they weren't my true feelings, but because I couldn't yet explain how I knew what I knew.

"Never mind."

"Oh no, you aren't getting out of this that easily." Shazer blocked my path. "Get talking."

I cleared my throat. "It's like—"

Bella rounded the corner, flushed and out of breath, saving me from explaining myself. "There you are. I've been looking all over for you."

"Take it things didn't go well with Finley?"

She shook her head. "She is . . . stubborn doesn't even begin to describe it. It is like she is blind to anything around her. Nothing I said got through, not a single word about my concerns."

"The ring?" I lifted an eyebrow.

Bella shook her head. "I'm sorry, I did try. I offered her my hand as we met, and she refused to take it. A clear offense if I didn't know why she refused."

Undines paused as they walked by, slowing to hear us. I put a hand on Bella's elbow. "Come, walk with me."

Shazer snorted. "This conversation is not done."

"Later," I said over my shoulder.

Bella talked as we strode through the street. "I think the same thing is happening to Finley that happened to me. It was almost like she *knows* we are here for the sapphire."

"Not possible; only the mother goddess knows." I turned sideways to let an Undine carrying a full basket of apples go by.

Bella glanced at me. "I knew what you wanted, the second you stepped into the dining hall."

I froze mid-stride. "Are you kidding me?"

"No. I knew without a shadow of a doubt that if I did not kill you, the ring would no longer be mine."

I was so screwed. Jaw ticking, I started forward again. "I need to figure out how we're going to get the stone then."

Bella pursed her lips and put two fingers to them, but said nothing.

"You still want to go to the library?" Peta asked.

"It's as good a place as any to plan," I said.

We followed her, but my mind was elsewhere.

Between the issue with getting the stone off Finley, Talan offering to train me, Ash missing, and the mystery of the old elemental . . . there was enough to keep me quiet. But that was not what made my mind roll in a loop over the events. No, it was the thought that the mother goddess was once again manipulating me. Asking me to retrieve the five stones, and then warning those who held them that I was coming.

Worm shit and green sticks, how the hell was I going to know if this was another game? And why would she warn them?

The answer was simple and unpleasant. I wouldn't know until it was too late to back out, until the game she played was done.

Peta trotted ahead of us, forcing Bella to hurry in order to keep up. We walked the halls, and for just a moment, I was taken back to our first visit to the Deep. To keeping Bella safe and fighting Requiem on behalf of Finley. The memories seemed to walk with me, rolling around like the fog that covered the Deep, keeping it safe from the humans.

Soon enough, we stood in front of a narrow, short set of doors. I lifted an eyebrow at Peta. "The Undines are not this short." I tapped the header of the door, which was at my eye level.

Peta shrugged. "Not an issue for me." She put her head against the door and pushed it open. A tang of salty air swept around me, air that hadn't been moved much. I peered in, seeing a young woman bent over a desk, holding a candle above a book that was at least two feet across.

I cleared my throat and she lifted a hand. "Come on in. Let me know if I can help you find anything."

Her voice tugged me closer to her and the memories

filled in the gaps. There was a flow to her body that reminded me of my niece, River. Of course she would have the same flow; she was River's half-sister.

"Stealing into the galley for food lately? Or is Finley turning out better than Requiem?" I asked.

Ray spun around, her hand going to her mouth. Her hair was as blue as her mother's had been, and her eyes as big and round as when she'd been a child. "Lark?" She looked past me. "Bella?" Then down. "Peta?"

I smiled at her and she flung herself at me, shocking me. Her arms tightened around me and just as fast she let go, and slammed the door shut, throwing a bar over it. "You shouldn't be here. Weird shit has been going on."

She hugged Bella, and ran a hand over Peta's head, but her eyes never left mine.

I raised both eyebrows. "Weird shit?"

She sat on a stool as she shook her head several times. "Finley is being . . . weird. I don't have any other word for it. Did you come to kick her off the throne? Like you did Requiem."

My turn to shake my head. "No." I glanced at Bella and gave another slight shake of my head. "I'm looking for some old papers."

Ray slumped in her chair. "Sure, I can help you with that. Even though it's rather boring."

I glanced at Peta. "Peta said you have some of the oldest records in all the elemental families, is that right?"

"Yes, though why they would keep them here is a mystery. With all the salt and moisture in the air, documents are hard to keep together."

"Unless someone wanted them to slowly disappear." Peta said exactly what I was thinking. I dropped a hand to her head, quieting her, but it was too late.

Ray's eyes widened. "Is this a mystery? Oh, please let me help. I'm bored out of my skull in here."

"No, not a mystery. Just an old story I'm looking into." The last thing I wanted was for Ray to get wrapped up in this mess. If things went badly with Finley and me, I didn't want anyone else to bear the brunt of the fallout.

The young Undine sighed. "Of course not. You know Sting became an Ender. They wouldn't allow me to try out. They said—"

"Not everyone can be a fighter," Bella said with a smile. "I had to learn that, too, that I was the diplomat, and my sister the fighter and protector of our family."

Her words shocked me. Never once had Bella indicated she was anything but happy with her lot in life, in being the diplomat. But maybe that was why she wanted to come with me.

Ray sighed again. "I know, I just . . . I just want an adventure, you know?"

"Be careful what you ask for," Peta said. "I used to want an adventure, and look what I got," she tipped her head toward me, "the biggest trouble maker of them all."

Ray and Bella laughed and I snorted.

"As lovely as it is to catch up, we have things we need to be doing," I said.

Ray stood. "Of course, I'm sorry." She beckoned for us to follow. We wove through barely balanced stacks of books that made up hallways. "We have a few things kept under sealed glass, but the oldest stuff is kept in the queen's chambers."

I glanced back at Peta who frowned, her tail twitching. "Under sealed glass there too?"

"No, it's not. Which is . . . weird again. Finley only just took the papers with her a few days ago. Prior to that, I wasn't even sure she knew the library existed. She sent others to gather anything she needed."

Ray stopped in front of a stack of books and touched the spine of a broken-down book in the middle. It scooted in and a door made up of books swung open. "Secret passage." She grinned at us.

The interior of the secret room was tight, and sparsely littered with papers in glass cases. I stepped farther into the room and Ray waved a hand. "There isn't much, but if it can help you, you're welcome to it."

Peta shifted into her housecat form and leapt up onto my shoulder. "I can see better from here."

"Which are the oldest ones?" I asked.

Ray nodded. "If you can describe the papers, I can help you find them quicker."

Peta tipped her head to one side. "The ones I remember were a small pile of notes, as if they'd been ripped out of a book, one edge torn up, the other rough. Handmade paper by the thickness, and the writing was in a pale gray ink."

"Most likely it started out black and faded." Ray bent over one of the glass cases. "I know the papers you speak of. They are here, I just cleaned the case yesterday." She flicked the edge of the case open, then frowned.

"Nothing?" I guessed.

Her frown deepened. "How did you know? They are gone. The queen must have taken them with the others. She is the only other one with knowledge of this place, even if she has never visited." She frowned. "Or I thought she didn't."

I rubbed a hand over my face, feeling things begin to spiral around us. "Bella, where was Finley headed after talking to you?"

Bella touched one of the papers under the glass. "I believe she was staying in the throne room. It looked as though she was dealing with supplicants."

The three of us left the tiny room and headed back to the main part of the library. "Ray, can you request for the papers to come back to you?"

"I can, but she can ignore me. She is the queen, after all. And it would take several days. Can you wait that long?" Her eyes were hopeful.

I shook my head. "No, I can't."

"Lark, does it not seem strange that those papers went missing on the day you arrived?" Peta asked.

I gave another sharp shake of my head. "No. Nothing in my life surprises me anymore. A damn elephant could show up and tell me he's a cousin and I wouldn't be shocked."

Ray laughed softly. "It can't be all that bad, can it?"

"Not bad," I muttered, "just—"

"No, it's bad." The white tip of Peta's tail flicked back and forth. "If the papers weren't important, she'd have never taken them. Which means you need them as much as you need to do that other thing."

Bella sighed. "I hate to agree, but I think Peta is right. Both are important. If she would hide them from you, then you need to find them."

"What other thing?" Ray perked up, but I already had my hands raised to stop her.

"No, you can't help."

Bella touched my arm. "What do you want to do?"

I tipped my head back to stare at the ceiling as if the answers would be written there. "Ray, I need you to forget we were here. If anyone asks, you don't know anything, you never saw us."

"Why?"
I looked at her.
"Because we're going to break into the queen's chambers."

CHAPTER 12

"This is a bad idea," I muttered as the three of us left Ray behind. The plan was to break into Finley's chambers, take the papers she'd hidden, then wait for Finley. We would surprise her, taking her down before she could react using the power of the sapphire.

No one would get hurt that way, and it wouldn't be a public trouncing of the Deep's queen. A win-win as far as I was concerned.

Right.

The hallways of the Deep were wide and tall and echoed my words. I clamped my lips shut as I strode forward. Confidence would take me further than looking like I was cringing. I did not want to steal from Finley, yet saw no other way to get the papers.

"It's your idea," Peta reminded me.

"It's *not* a bad idea," Bella said. "Surprising her might be the only way to get the sapphire without a battle."

I wasn't so sure, but I had nothing else, no other idea. And since she wasn't the Finley I remembered, then maybe it was okay. I could almost see Ash shake his head at me, his gold eyes half shuttered and a wry smile on his lips. The image lightened the fears in me. Peta glanced up and raised both eyebrows.

"What can possibly make you smile at this moment?"

I shrugged. "Ash."

Frowning, she turned her head forward again. "You think he would agree with this decision."

Bella laughed. "He would. Just as I would and you do, Peta. We have all learned the hard way that Lark's ideas are often the only way. Even if her ideas are the ones that scare us the most."

Finley's quarters were in the center of the Deep, not far from the throne room. I followed the curving hallway, thinking of how best to handle this. In the end, I knew there was only going to be one way and someone was going to get hurt.

A sigh escaped me and again Peta looked up at me. "It will never be easy for you, Lark."

"Doesn't mean I have to like it." The three of us rounded the gentle curve in the hallway and Finley's quarters were in front of us. How did I know? An Ender stood to each side of the door, both holding tridents, both wearing full-face armor so I had no idea if they were even Enders I knew. Like Dolph. Or young Sting. I'd really hoped one of them would be the Ender I had to deal with. Shit sticks, I hated those weapons of theirs. With their reach, they were as hard to fight as any spear, but with the barbs at the end, they were deadly if they pierced skin.

"Think I can talk my way through?"

"Yes, but are you willing to risk your soul? It's already sliding; I don't recommend using Spirit," Peta said.

I wasn't really eager to use it either. Spirit was not something I'd ever truly understood; mostly it came to me in moments of sheer desperation. Or anger. Neither of which I had going for me at the moment.

Bella took a step. "Let me try."

She led the way, lifting a hand in greeting. "Is Finley in? I would like to speak to her."

They tightened their holds on their respective tridents, lowering them toward us. The one on the left shifted his stance, widening his legs. "The queen has given orders to keep everyone away from her chambers."

We drew closer, even as Bella nodded. "Of course. Could one of you take a message for me? I wish to apologize and ask her forgiveness."

Peta's shoulders twitched, and I managed to keep my face neutral. Harmless.

Lefty snorted. "Do I look like a messenger boy?"

Bella smiled as sweetly as I'd ever seen her. "No. But I thought because I said please you'd do it. Please."

He brought his trident down so the points hovered at her chest. "I suggest you leave, Terraling."

So we were back to that. I pulled Bella away, so fast she spun, and he shifted so the trident now faced me. I touched a finger to the middle point of the three-pronged weapon. "Really? You want to play that game with me, little boy?"

He pulled back, his body tensing. I dropped to the floor as the trident shot through where my chest had been. I kicked him in the knees, breaking one by the feel of the bones crunching. I rolled out of his way as he fell, grabbed his trident and jerked it from his hands. I spun and blocked the second Ender as he swept toward me. The tridents locked and I twisted mine hard to the right, jerking his from his hands.

When it came to strength, as a Terraling, I had it hands down against any of the other elemental families. Score one for the elemental built like a brick shithouse.

He leaned over me, bringing his face nice and close, a short sword in his hand.

With the trident out of the way, and still on my back, I kicked up and nailed him in the jaw under his helmet. His head snapped back and he fell in a boneless heap, his head clanging on the stone floor. Rolling to my belly, I stared into the eyes of Lefty. I reached out and yanked his helmet off.

He was a kid, young and probably not even finished with his Ender training.

"Don't kill me," he whispered, terror in his eyes.

I snaked a hand out and circled my fingers around his neck. I pulled him close to me as I squeezed down on the arteries. He scrabbled at my hand, and then slowly went limp.

I stood, dropped the trident, grabbed a leg on each Ender and hurried to the door. "Not much time. Bella, get the door."

"How are we going to get Finley here?" She held the door open for me and I dragged the two Enders into Finley's room.

The room was done in soft pastel colors that mimicked the ocean and the white sandy beaches. I wanted to stop and look, to take it in because there was a peace in the room I hadn't felt in a long time. Not since before I'd been banished. I realized it was the same sensation I'd picked up in the Eyrie. A sense of belonging.

Child of spirit, you will find your home in all places.

I froze, swallowed hard, and looked around. That was the same voice I'd heard in the mountains right before I destroyed the Eyrie. I hoped it was not a precursor to what was coming.

I shook it off, rolled the two Enders off to one side and followed Peta as she sniffed the air. "This way, I can smell the salty musty papers."

"Lark, how are we going to get Finley here?" Bella asked again.

I glanced at her. "If she knows I'm here for the sapphire, she'll find me, I think. Whoever is controlling her doesn't like me much and seems to think I can be taken out. I'm banking on that arrogance."

Peta trotted through the room to a door set into the wall that would have been easy to miss. The wall was covered in sand that shifted under my hand when I touched it, the warm granules all but vibrating under my touch.

Bella moved up beside me. "You are putting a lot of weight on mere possibilities."

"I don't want to fight Finley if I don't have to. She's a good queen, and once upon a time, she was a good friend to us both."

The edge of the door shimmered and showed itself as I passed my hand over it. Pressing against it, I was surprised when the door slid inward, opening up into a glass dome, one of the sparkling tower tops seen from the water.

"You say that like . . ." Bella trailed off, took a breath. "Like you would kill her if you faced her."

"If I have to, I will. Because if I don't and Blackbird gets a hold of that stone, we are going to have to face him. And I know he is stronger than me even without the stones. Better that she die, than you and me." I stepped into the small room and leaned over a table where three pieces of paper lay and chose to ignore the horrified silence from my sister.

The papers were ancient. So heavily salt-encrusted, the words were barely legible. They lay in a shaft of sunlight coming in through the dome. A faint breeze from the ocean floated through. As though they were placed deliberately to disintegrate under the weather.

Bella and I leaned over them, and Peta stood up on her back legs to peer at the papers.

"Can you read them?"

Bella nodded. "It's very old script. You two keep watch, I'll read."

I put a hand on her shoulder and turned.

At least I was right about one thing. Finley had found me, though I'd hoped we'd have more time.

Her blue eyes flashed with anger and the blue stone on her finger caught the light. Damn it, I was in trouble. With the blue sapphire, Finley had access to even more power within water, and more speed.

I had to end this fast.

"Peta, stay with Bella."

"Lark—"

"Please."

She let out a pitiful mew and hurried back into the room. I pulled my spear from my side, linking the two pieces together.

"Finley, I am leaving, and I'm taking the ring with me. I don't want to hurt you, so please give it to me."

"You think you can face me when I wear this?" She lifted her hand, a haughty look in her eye. That was not the girl I'd known. Damn the sapphire, and damn me for giving it to her.

The bed to the right of me shimmered and water spilled up and out of it. Shit sticks, this was going to get ugly fast if I didn't do something.

"Bella, stay where you are!"

Gritting my teeth, I pulled the spear back and threw it at Finley. I didn't want to hit her, only wanted to distract her. The spear shot forward, to the left of her head. She jerked away, her eyes wide.

She might be a ruler, but a true fighter she was not.

I leapt at her while she was distracted, tackling her to the ground. If I could knock her out we'd be gone before she woke up. Sure, she'd be pissed as hell, but when had that stopped me before?

Finley rolled with me across the floor as she flicked her one hand at me. Lines of power raced along her skin and I clamped my mouth shut. The water from the bed roared out and filled the room in a matter of seconds. Finley floated in front of me, a smug smile on her lips. Again, not something I'd ever attributed to her.

I swam for her and she easily dodged me. There was no choice, I had to tap into the earth or Peta, Bella, and I were dead. I held my hand out to the wall where the sand gathered and beckoned it forward. Spirit and Earth roared through my mind and I fought it, focusing on what I had to do. Balance. Talan had said it was about balance.

Easy to think, not so easy to put into practice. The sand floated through the water to me. Finley threw her head back, laughing soundlessly. I pulled the sand together, crushing it into a tight bond so it became shards of glass. Staring at Finley's middle finger where the ring rested, I prepped my aim.

Power roared through me as I flicked my fingers toward her hand. The shards of glass shot forward, slicing through the water and into her finger. Blood spurted in a pink bloom and her finger fell, floating side to side.

I swam forward and grabbed the finger, and the ring. Gripping the ring, I felt the pull of the ocean and sent the water in the room to it. A ripple ran through my body, like the water took a part of me with it as it left. I slumped to the floor, gasping for air as I looked for Peta and Bella.

Sodden, and in her snow leopard form, Peta stepped out of the smaller room first. Bella was right behind her, gasping for air as well, green lines of power hovering over her arms.

"Easy, Bella. It's done," I said. I pushed myself to my feet, and glanced at Finley who clutched her hand to her. "I'm sorry, Finley, but I can't leave this with you."

I backed away, and Peta hurried to my side.

Finley lifted her head, her blue eyes watering. "Wait, Lark, please wait! I can't rule without the ring. I'm not strong enough."

"You are, but you'll never know it as long as you wear this." I pulled the ring from the finger.

"There was a voice in my head, I couldn't stop what he wanted."

Finley's words sent a shiver down my spine and I paused in mid-stride. "Who?"

"I don't know." Her whole body shook. "I couldn't stop what I was doing. I sent that assassin to kill you. I know I did. But I didn't want to. The voice made me." She burst into tears.

I glanced at Peta, unsure of what to do. The words didn't feel like a lie, and Finley sounded more like herself than she had since we'd been in the Deep.

Bella went to her side. "The same thing happened to

me. The stones are dangerous, and Lark is making sure this doesn't happen again."

Finley looked up at her, still clutching her wounded hand. "Lark was the one who gave it to me."

I grimaced, Talan's words once more making themselves known. "I didn't know what they were. I thought they were best to be kept in the hands of those who understood the power."

A shudder rippled through her. "I ache for the stone. Give it to me, for a moment."

"No." I took a step back. The need in her eyes was something akin to the human addicts I'd come across in the few human cities I'd been in. A desire so fierce, it overcame all common sense. Bella kept a hand on her.

"Easy, Finley. It will pass."

A clatter of feet in the hallway snapped me around. I grabbed my spear from where it was buried in the wall. I dropped to a knee on one side of Finley and Bella as three Enders arrived, one of them Dolph.

She held a hand to them. "No, she has done no wrong. I think she may have saved us. Again." Her blue eyes lifted to mine. "Lark, you have cleared my mind of his commands."

"Who though? Who commanded you?"

She leaned into Bella, putting her head on my sister's shoulder. I took her injured hand, knowing I could heal her. Wondering if I should, if the cost to my own soul was worth it.

Damn, if I wouldn't heal her, I was losing whatever good was in me. I pulled her bloody hand out and covered it with my own. My body shook as I pulled on Spirit, weaving it through her wound and closing it. I let her go and she held up her hand, her eyes wide.

"Lark, I didn't know you could do that."

Peta butted her head between us. "To truly destroy, you have to know how to heal first."

Her words seemed to shimmer in the air, and that same shiver I'd felt before crawled up my spine. The words were too close to me, too close to the truth I was learning, and I waved my hand as if to bat them away.

"Finley, who commanded you to try and kill me?"

She put her healed hand—minus one finger—to her forehead. "I don't know. The voice was familiar and he made me do things. I think . . . I think you are right, it has to do with the ring." Her eyes flicked to my closed fist. "Take it away, Lark. I don't want it anywhere near me." Finley pushed my closed hand away. "I don't have the strength to hang onto it and not use it, even though I know I will be manipulated. I want the power too much."

"You see?" Bella said. "Already you are clearing from it."

Finley's body shook. "I used it sparingly, though I wore it often. Perhaps . . . that is why it already fades from my mind."

I stood and held a hand out to her. She put her hand in mine and I pulled her to her feet. She wrapped an arm around my waist. "I'm sorry I turned on you, my friend."

"No apology needed." I gave her a squeeze and let her go. "But we must leave." I pushed away from her. The chance we'd make it to Fiametta and Samara before Blackbird was slipping away from me.

"Wait!"

I paused and looked back.

"You are seeking Ash, aren't you?"

Staring at her, I wasn't sure I'd heard her right. Her words couldn't have stolen the air from my lungs more completely if she was Sylph. "What?"

"Ash, I saw him right before he went missing . . ." She shuddered. "He was looking for Cassava and he thought he'd find her in the cypress swamps. That was where he went. I did not remember until you healed my hand, like it healed a part of my mind that was meant not to recall."

"Thank you for telling me." The cypress swamps. I tucked the piece of information into the back of my mind. I would go after Ash if I thought I could find him on my own, but I knew I had to deal with the stones first, before Blackbird could get his hands on them.

Finley nodded, pulled her shoulders straight and swept past me, snapping her fingers at Dolph. "I want a proper report of the Deep within the hour for the past six months. I have been controlled for the last time." There was more than anger in her voice; a low simmering rage radiated off her.

He bent at the waist and raised grateful eyes to me. "It will be done, my Queen."

I nodded at him as I went by and he touched the top of my hand in a gesture I'd not seen since I'd been in the Pit. A sign of respect; one he gave to both Bella and Peta as well.

I followed Finley, catching up to her easily. Which turned out to be fortuitous for her.

As we circled around a corner, two Sylphs approached, their strides as long as the rest of them, their movement anything but friendly as their hands went to their weapons. Their long white hair and white leathers marked them as Enders for their people. Fighters and enforcers.

The hallway we stood in groaned as a hard wind curled through it, tugging at the tapestries and painting that hung above us.

"Why am I not surprised?" I pushed Finley and Bella behind me as I snapped my spear out, holding it in front of me to bar them.

The Sylphs held up their hands in tandem and the wind picked up, howling as though a hurricane had been unleashed within the Deep. "Peta, take the left."

She leapt in front of me in her snow leopard form. She raced ahead, her body close to the ground.

Finley flicked a hand and from below the Sylphs, the Deep rumbled. "Finley, I can't breathe under water."

"With the ring you can!"

Hell, I did not want to put the ring on. What if I was controlled? But she was right, it would at least allow me to breathe water as though I were an Undine. And maybe I'd hear the voice try to tell me what to do.

"Peta, find high ground. Bella, get back!"

Peta skidded and leapt for an open window. Finley snapped her fingers and the hallway flooded between one breath and the next, filling to the rafters, but never spilling through the windows or doors, like a self-contained aquarium. At the edge, I saw Bella pacing and Finley with her hands held out holding the water steady.

I slid the ring on and took a breath. The Sylphs would have no problem breathing with their connection to air, but they fumbled in the water. I swam toward them, my spear clutched in one hand as they tried to backpedal.

I grabbed the foot of the Sylph closest to me, yanking him through the water so we were eye level. He swept a hand toward me, the glittering edge of his knife cutting through the water with ease. I caught his wrist against my arm, spun my hand and grabbed his hand. With a sharp twist I broke several of his fingers and the knife fell.

Arms snaked around me from behind, as the Sylph in front of me kicked out, nailing me in the stomach. A burst of air bubbled out of my mouth, but didn't float away. As

I struggled to breathe, the bubbles hovered in front of me. They floated closer until they pressed against my eyes.

Air pressure and eyes. Not a good combination as far as I was concerned.

I jerked hard, loosening the hold on me, but not breaking free entirely. The air bubbles flitted around my face, pressing against my cheeks as they slid closer to my eyes.

Worm shit and green sticks, this was not going well.

Kicking backward, I caught the Sylph in the family jewels, and his hold disappeared. The Sylph in front of me drove his knife at my face, the blade's edge so close I knew I couldn't dodge it.

I jerked my head backward, already knowing it would too be slow, that the knife would cut across my eyes.

He was yanked down and back, the blade going with him. Below him, Peta had her jaws clamped around his ankle as she bit down, pink swirls of blood flowing from the wound.

I swung backward without looking, using the full length of my spear. It buried into a body and I yanked it forward. Peta wouldn't have long before she needed air. I spun in a circle and saw Finley and Bella arguing by the way their hands were moving. The Sylph I'd dropped was injured, but still alive as he floated downward, his eyes closed with pain.

Perfect. I swam forward and grabbed the Sylph Peta had in her jaws. Holding him by the throat with one hand, I drove my spear through his heart with the other. His body convulsed, blood spilled into the clear blue water and his eyes fogged over. Bubbles raced from his mouth and this time they did as they should have, floating up above our heads.

I let him go and gripped the blue stone. With a quick gesture I sent the water out the windows.

It dropped in a rush, and I belatedly realized Peta and I were going with it.

I reached for her, barely catching her by the tip of her long tail. I tapped into Earth and pulled us toward the tile floor even as the power fought me, bucking against the hold I had on it. The spire around us trembled, the sandstone cracking under the pressure. As soon as our feet touched I let go of Earth, but Spirit was having none of it. "Bella, help me!"

She raised her arms and her power collided with mine. The stone around us groaned, but held steady as I brought Spirit to me and eased off on my connection to the earth. I lifted a hand. "Good enough."

Peta pressed her body against mine, her fur plastered to her frame. "What is it about you and water?"

"Damned if I know," I muttered. I spat, trying to clear out the taste of salt water. Finley sat across from us on a bench, the Sylph on his knees in front of her as he clutched his side.

"He won't speak, Lark. Can you help?" Finley's voice was as sweet as I'd ever heard it.

If I were the Sylph, I'd be worried.

I pushed to my feet and moved to stand beside her. The Sylph wouldn't look at me. He could have still fought. His power was strong enough that there was no doubt he could have battled us with the water gone. But he didn't, which was strange.

"You were sent to kill the queen?"

He rolled his eyes and drew a slow breath but didn't answer.

"So you were sent to kill me?"

His jaw tightened.

Bingo.

I cringed thinking about using Spirit so soon after it fought me. Bile rolled in my guts and I had to force my hand to settle on his forearm. I sent a pulse of Spirit through him, clearing out any connection he would have had to another Spirit user.

He glared up at me.

"He's not under any compulsion. Which means he's here on orders." I slumped against the wall, struggling to speak around the need to lie down and close my eyes. Each time I used my connections to the earth or Spirit, the struggle worsened. In that Talan was right; soon enough I would lose control completely.

I knew my limits, and I was fast approaching them.

Finley tapped a finger to her chin. "How could they even know you were here? And why would Samara send assassins after you?"

I wasn't entirely sure they were only after me. "If they could have killed you, the Deep would be in upheaval again. You have no obvious heir to the throne."

"But what would that do to help Samara?" Finley shook her head. "It makes no sense."

In that I had to agree. I couldn't see what Samara hoped to gain by attacking Finley.

Peta cleared her throat. "Finley, may I ask him a question?"

The young queen nodded. "If you think he will answer."

She trotted in front of the Sylph and sat down. "You are an Ender, so you are trained to withstand interrogation so I will not ask why you are here. I only wish to know if your queen still wears a gift we gave her. A sign of peace. The smoky diamond?"

He grunted, his lips curling downward. "There is no peace between us, so while she wears it still, do not count it in your favor."

Clever, clever cat. I ran a hand over her head. "Peta, you are a gem."

"Oh, I know." She winked up at me, and Bella smirked, though she covered it with a hand.

The smoky diamond was the stone that controlled air, giving its wearer more power, as the blue sapphire had done for Finley and water. So whoever was controlling Finley was also controlling Samara. And that was the true enemy. The one behind the stones.

"I'd throw him in the dungeon until you know more," I said. The dungeons of the Deep blocked an elemental's ability to touch their power, rendering them useless.

Almost like a human.

Dolph and three more Undine Enders bolted into the hallway. "What the hell happened?"

Finley smiled. "We took care of it. Take this Sylph to the dungeons, Dolph. I will question him later. And send a healer to him, I don't want him dead. Yet."

The Sylph twisted in her hands and whipped out a short knife. Everyone was too far away; he had a perfect shot at Finley.

I lunged for her, my instinct to protect overriding any sense of self-preservation. But the Sylph didn't swing at the queen.

He twisted the handle around and drove the knife into his own heart. His body convulsed and blood bubbled out of his mouth and over his chin. With a final breath, he slumped to his knees and fell back onto the sandstone, blood pooling around him.

"Damn." Dolph looked from Finley to me, and back to Finley again. "I've noticed there's only trouble when Lark shows up. Perhaps her visits should be shorter."

I grimaced. "We are leaving, right now."

"Dry clothes first," Bella said.

Finley stood next to me. "I can fix that." She snapped her fingers, blue lines swallowing her hand. The moisture leapt from her clothes and hair, leaving her as dry as if she'd never been in the water. I raised an eyebrow at her and she snapped her fingers at Peta, Bella, and me.

The moisture whipped off me, hanging in the air in front of my face in a thousand tiny droplets before splashing to the floor. Finley did the same for Bella, whose skirts moved loose around her legs once more, a puddle of water at her feet. I glanced down at Peta and burst out laughing. She had the most water at her paws, but her hair was fluffed up as if she'd been in a windstorm for three days running.

Frowning, she glared at me. "Not funny."

Finley laughed softly. With a gentle wave of her hand, Peta's hair smoothed back down. "I took too much water is all; that should be better." Her words set off a riot of thoughts in my brain.

Too much water. Too much air. Too much spirit and earth. Too much of every element, and yet . . . there was something missing.

I felt as though I was on the edge of understanding something vital to my survival. And yet, once more, it slipped away from me.

Close, child, you draw close to the truth. Be ready for its violence.

I tightened my jaw to keep from responding, because what would I say? Whatever the voice was, I knew the truth was far harder than the lies. That had been my entire life.

CHAPTER 13

inley went with us to the stable to gather Shazer. "I want to see you off."

"You mean you want to make sure we don't cause more problems?" I laughed, but even I heard the bitter notes in it.

Finley shook her head. "No, Dolph is right. You have a knack for uncovering the darkness in our world, Lark."

I grimaced. "Yeah, I've noticed that too."

Peta sat on my shoulder, once more in her housecat form. "The issue is that the news of something happening here that involved Lark will get to the other rulers before we can. Is the ambassador from the Pit still here?"

Finley raised a hand. "Dolph, can you answer this?"

He strode to her right side. "He left last night, shortly after Lark arrived."

I shook my head. "It doesn't matter, not really. The stones are used as a form of compulsion. Whoever is using them already knows I'm on the hunt for them. The ambassador will only confirm I'm on my way." I could only hope that meant Blackbird would also be stalled. Or that he started searching after me, and followed rather than beat me to the other rulers. Who was I kidding? Certainly not myself; Blackbird was hunting as actively as I was. I'd just been lucky so far. Which meant we had to keep moving.

We stopped on the white beach, and Shazer went to one knee. Bella mounted and I leapt up behind her. "Be safe, Finley."

She raised her hand. "You have my word, Lark. I will not be fooled again."

Before I could answer, Shazer took off, galloping down the beach and gaining speed; right at the edge of the water he leapt. His hooves skimmed the surface and a dark torpedo-shaped body glimmered underneath us. I shuddered and looked away. We were done with the Deep.

It was the next family I needed to focus on.

Shazer glanced back at me. "Eyrie or Pit?"

Neither choice left me with much hope, but at least with the Salamanders, I'd left on good terms. Not so much for the Eyrie, seeing as how I'd destroyed their home.

"Pit. We leave the Eyrie for last and hope we have enough by then to take Samara down easily."

Shazer snorted. "The Sylphs never go down easily."

I thought about the two Enders who'd tried to kill Finley and me. "No, they don't. Which means the more stones I can collect before I face her, the better. Not that the Pit is going to be an easy in and out."

Bella looked back at me. "But is that not true of Fiametta? You have two rings already. Could you not use them to take her down?"

"The Pit is on an active volcano which Fiametta has

direct control over. I'm not sure that going in swinging with all the power at our fingertips is a good idea."

"Then what's the plan?" Shazer banked to one side, angling us west across the continent.

"I'm hoping Peta can help me with that," I said. Peta looked up at me from my lap.

"What do you need?"

"Your first charge, Talan. He was a Spirit Elemental. I need you to tell me all the things he could do."

Her tiny eyebrows shot up. "You think you can learn without training? I told you I would take you to him when you were ready."

She had, and I'd almost forgotten that. "Do you think I'm ready?"

"No, you are not. You're too stubborn to learn from him, and he is too stubborn to teach you."

Bella laughed. "Why don't you tell her how you really feel, Peta?"

Peta shrugged. "You aren't ready. I can't even describe how I know, only that I *know*."

The wind whipped around us, an errant current that tugged at our hair and pulled us to one side of Shazer's back. He grunted and angled with the wind to correct it. I twisted in my seat to scan the sky around us. No Sylph waited behind or below us.

"Sometimes an element is just an element, Lark," Peta said.

It was my turn to laugh. "But when it's not, it's damn deadly."

Peta smiled up at me. "True. Back to your question. I don't think I can tell you all the things he did. They didn't have names to me, he didn't explain himself. He didn't tell me anything, really."

"You've helped me before," I pointed out.

"And you would have my help now if I could do anything!" She curled against me. "It's not that I don't want to help, it's that I don't think I can."

Bella's eyes met mine, and in them I saw the confusion I felt. Peta was not like this. I held a hand out to my familiar. "Give me your paw."

"No."

I grabbed her by the scruff before she could worm away from me and took one of her paws in my hand. Her tiny claws dug into me, but the skin of her pad brushed against mine.

I felt the shattering of Spirit's hold on her as our skin touched.

She stared up at me, horror in her eyes. "I couldn't help myself. I was told not to help you, to let you figure things out on your own."

I nodded, anger snapping through me. "Do you know who did it?"

She shook her head. "No."

"I do." I took a breath. "Talan met with me in the Deep. He was the one who left the bracelet, he was the reason I was acting strange. He . . . didn't want you to know he'd been there."

Grief and pain sliced through the bond between Peta and me. She tucked her head against my belly as if to hide her shame. "Why would he do that?"

I shook my head, placing a hand on her back. "I don't know. It's a game to him, I think, as it is to whoever is using the stones."

My words seemed to still the air and Bella's eyes widened. "Could it be him doing all this? Could he be playing both sides?"

Slowly, I nodded. "He controls Spirit, and he's been around a long time." The puzzle pieces cleared in front of me. Bella's words were closer to the truth than I think even she realized.

Peta shook her head. "No, I can't believe he'd do this. That he'd try to kill you."

"Unless he wanted you back as a familiar, unless he wanted the stones for himself and thought to take them from me once I gathered them." I recalled all too well the sadness in him when he spoke of Peta loving me better than him. I tightened my hold on her, as if by sheer will alone I'd be able to keep her with me.

I told them everything he'd said about me being trained. I said nothing about the battle, or how he'd said I'd screwed up. Or how he'd said Peta loved me better. I wasn't so sure, and I didn't think I could bear to hear her lie to me. My heart couldn't handle knowing she was never truly mine.

Two days of flying took us across the continent to the eastern side of the Pacific Ocean. We spoke mostly of inconsequential things. Things that would mean nothing to anyone else, and yet they allowed me to freely consider other thoughts and possibilities . . . other ideas that could explain how the rulers knew we were coming.

Though I could easily blame the mother goddess, I doubted she would give me a charge, only to sabotage me. Not when it was clear that she truly believed the stones had to be gathered, and quickly before Blackbird gained hold of them. That left the creator of the stones, and Talan. And I was beginning to believe they were one and the same. The timing was too coincidental that he would appear in my life when the issue with the stones arose.

So his game with me in the Deep was just that, a ruse to throw me off. But how in a bucket of goblin piss had Finley and Bella known I was there before I'd ever revealed myself? Talan found me; could he somehow be tracking me? There were no Trackers left in the world so I knew that was out. The knowing of my impending presence had the feel of stepping into a trap I had no idea was even there.

We swept through the skies high above the Pit and I still had no answer as to how the rulers were being alerted to my presence.

"You've got a plan?" Shazer asked.

"Yes, though it will depend on my ability to control Spirit and Earth together." I stared down at the mountain that held the Pit in its belly, smoke curling out of the top of it. About halfway down the mountain was an indent. Not a cave, but a section that had collapsed, leaving a lip of rock sticking out. "See that edge there; can you drop me off?"

"I can do you one better and land there." Shazer tipped his wings and angled us toward the mountain. With a swift backstroke, he slowed our descent and landed us on the edge with a soft bump.

I slid from his back and went to my knees, pressing my hands to the dirt, knowing time was of the essence. "Everyone else stay on Shazer's back. If this doesn't work I want you out of here fast."

Peta leapt to my shoulder, in complete defiance of what I'd just said. I opened my mouth to argue with her, and then stopped. I reached a hand up. "Rebel cat."

"Loyal, not rebellious." She tightened her hold on me.

Carefully, I opened myself to my connection to the earth first. It hummed around me, filling me with power before I called on it. Teeth gritted, I reached for my connection with Spirit.

The element writhed inside me, lashing to be let loose. "Damn it."

The mountain rumbled and the stones around us hopped with the vibration. I swallowed hard and focused all my energy on what I was doing. Whatever balance I'd had was gone and the two elements within me seemed to know it.

The mountain shimmied again despite my efforts to keep it still.

Worm shit, this was going downhill faster than I'd thought possible. I only needed to find the Firewyrms. From there, I was sure they could help me find an entranceway that wasn't guarded. At least not by Fiametta's people. Spirit wove around Earth and my power sank into the mountain. I closed my eyes as a shudder rippled through me, not unlike the strange pleasure I'd felt in the graveyard when Talan had stared at me.

But this time, it was my own connection to Spirit that caught the edges of the unwelcome sensation. Muscles clenched, I pushed past it. Through the mountain I sent my power, searching for the creatures that lived alongside the Salamanders. Finally, in the deepest depths of the Pit, I touched on a soul I knew.

Scar. The first Firewyrm I'd ever met. Though he was older now, he lifted his head as my power rolled over him. I sent him a simple command.

Come to me.

In the depths, I felt him move toward us. I withdrew Spirit and Earth, bringing them back to heel easier than I'd thought was going to happen. Balance was what Talan said. What was it I'd done that was so different than before?

The answer was there, just at the edge of my mind, only I couldn't quite reach it. Damn.

I stood and brushed my hands off. "Now we wait."

"Why not just tunnel your way in?" Shazer asked.

"And end up inside the Pit because we took a wrong turn? I think not." I folded my arms.

Minutes ticked by. Bella made a move as if to slide off Shazer. "No, stay there. Please."

"I thought you were calling up a friend?" She frowned and I shrugged.

"People change. He was a friend, but it has been a lot of years."

"Someone is coming." Shazer snorted, and stamped a foot.

The section of mountain next to us crumbled and stones fell in a trickle around my knees, but I didn't move. A flash of white scales behind the tumbling dirt caught my eye, and then Scar poked his head out of a hole twelve feet high and wide. He'd made a perfect circular opening, big enough that even Shazer would be able to pass with his wings tucked back.

"Larkspur?"

"Hello, Scar."

His tongue flicked out and he looked past me to Shazer and Bella. "What are you doing here? And why aren't you coming in through the front door?"

"I need a different way in, one Fiametta doesn't know about. She's not happy with me right now." I looked around him. "This would do nicely, I think."

He snorted and shook his head, the horns that curled

back over his neck brushing against the top of the tunnel he'd made. "Then perhaps I should not let you in. The queen has been our champion since you left, keeping us safe. Allowing us to stay behind when you would call us to battle."

His tongue snaked out again, and his eyes narrowed. I took a step. "The world was in danger, and you turned away. Don't think I feel sorry for your scaly ass."

So maybe that wasn't the best way to deal with him when we needed his help, but when the Firewyrms had declined to stand with us in the battle against Orion and the demons, I'd been shocked. I'd saved them once, and as far as I was concerned, they owed me.

A snarl rolled out of him. "You know nothing, Elemental. When you left, our people were healthy, and we had a future ahead of us. When the demons were loosed, the sickness they spread," he shook his head, "it wiped our numbers down to only a few. If we went to battle, we might have been completely wiped out."

Shame flickered and died before it ever took root. I shook my head. "You mean like the rest of the supernaturals who fought when there were only a few left? There are species that are extinct now, and those who are on the cusp of it. Do not bemoan to me that you only had a few numbers. Everyone was in the same position, and yet they came. You did not."

He hunched his shoulders and I raised my hand. "It is the past already. No more. Will you allow me to use this entrance?"

The pause was heavy and weighted with things unsaid.

"Please don't bring the mountain down on us."

"I would never—" I clamped my mouth shut, rephrased my words and tried again. "I will do my best."

He snorted softly, but retreated, allowing us access to the opening. "I will let you in for the good you did before. If not for that, I would never allow you to step foot in here."

I glanced at Bella and gave her a quick nod. She slid from Shazer's back, and pointed a finger at me. "Do not even try to tell me to wait for you."

"Would never dream of it." I stepped into the tunnel. I knew when I could win an argument with her, and when I would have my reasoning handed back to me in pieces. This was one of the latter times.

Scar waited patiently, his scales lighting up the darkness like a giant firefly. I opened my mouth to ask him a question about the feel of the Pit and Fiametta's current state of mind, and closed it just as swiftly. He was not the friend I remembered. I could almost see the change in him, as if it were imprinted on his scales.

As Bella stepped in I looked back to Shazer, his body silhouetted by the bright blue sky.

"Not a chance in hell will I step in there." He flicked his head once. "I will be close by."

"Good enough. Keep an eye out for us." I put a hand on Bella, stopping her. "Close the opening."

Her eyes widened. "Do you think that's wise?"

"I trust Scar enough to see us through this. And if anyone notices a giant hole in the side of the mountain, whatever surprise we might have will be lost."

The concern on her face was obvious, but she did as I asked. Peta whispered in my ear, her curiosity getting the better of her. "Why didn't you do it?"

The thoughts that had woven through my mind during the previous two days finally came to light, and at last I was able to grasp the idea firmly.

"I don't know if it's possible, but what if the person who controls the stones can detect those who use elemental powers nearby? And if he can do that much, perhaps he can tell who those people are that use them."

"It isn't Talan." Peta tightened her hold on me. "I know you don't trust him, and I don't understand what he is doing, but I know he would not want to harm you."

I wanted to believe her, but the reality was that she hadn't been with him as his familiar in a long, long time. People changed with time and the harsh realities of life.

I was proof enough of that.

"Unless I have to, I won't use my connection to Earth or Spirit again. Already it may be too late. The thought didn't come to me until now."

Bella finished closing the opening and the darkness tightened around us. She hurried to my side, and took hold of my hand. "Don't let go."

I smiled at her. "Never."

Hand in hand, as though we were children afraid of the dark, we followed Scar through the tunnel.

The Firewyrm was quiet, except for the sound of his long claws scraping along the floor. He led us in a looping spiral downward, the heat rising with each step until sweat ran down my cheeks, drying before it could drip off the edge of my jaw.

Bella wasn't doing much better. Her cheeks were flushed and her hair stuck to her skin wherever it touched her.

It wasn't long before we were deep within the mountain, the feeling of it all around us, pressing down.

Reminding me all too closely of my time trapped.

Buried and forgotten.

I shivered, fighting the roll of nausea that whispered

through me. I would not vomit, I would not. My guts heaved and I shook at the effort to keep my food where it belonged.

Scar stopped in front of us, and his body rippled, as though he were suddenly inundated with ants, and the faintest lines of pink rolled over him.

Worm shit and green sticks.

Someone was using Spirit on the Firewyrm, instructing him.

And the intention behind the command was anything but friendly.

CHAPTER 14

"Hang on!" I tightened my hold on Bella and dove toward the wall on our right. Connecting with the mountain, I pulled the power of the earth around me and opened the stone face and shoved Bella in. "Stay there. I can't protect us both."

"Wait!" She held a hand out, but stayed where I'd put her. "Lark, duck!"

I spun and dropped to my belly as Scar's tail flung over my head. His eyes were full of tears as he stared at me. "I cannot stop myself, Lark. I'm sorry."

He lunged again, his mouth wide, his fangs as big as my forearm. I rolled to the left, and one of his fangs nicked my right shoulder. A searing pain sliced through me, the same fire that had been the lava whip against my bare skin, the same burn that had nearly killed me. I grounded myself to the mountain and let the strength of the earth keep me on my feet though I swayed as though poisoned.

I spun my spear off my side and pointed it at him. Though it was puny looking next to his mouth full of razor-sharp teeth, he paused.

"Scar, fight it." I didn't lower the spear.

"I can't," he said, his voice the same soft gentle voice I'd known before. He lunged so fast there would be no dodging him. His mouth was wide, tongue flicking the air.

Peta leapt from my shoulder, shifting in mid-air.

Taking my place.

Protecting me with her own body.

"NO!"

Scar's mouth snapped shut, reflexes kicking in the second Peta touched the inside of his mouth as though he were a crocodile. She disappeared, as he clamped down, as if she never was.

Peta was gone and along with her went any coherent thought passing through my mind.

Screaming, I ran at him, driving him back with each sweeping pass of my spear. He dodged me as if I were nothing. Over and over again I attacked, and he didn't even blink at my attempts. My spear bounced off his thick hide, not because it wasn't sharp, but because I wasn't strong enough to actually make it pierce.

Who cared if I saved the world, if I saved Ash even, if I lost Peta?

I tapped into both Spirit and Earth, weaving them together into a deadly mix of power. The two elements raced through me, firing my blood, feeding my strength and reflexes. I ran at the side wall, ran partway up, and leapt off twisting in the air, landing on top of Scar's back. He bucked and writhed under me, but I clamped my legs tightly and kept my seat.

Bella waved from the ground. "More Firewyrms."

Peta, I had to get Peta. I had to believe she was not dead, that somehow she was okay. I couldn't feel my bond to her, my panic and fear driving away all thought, all consideration except to save her.

I raised my hand and the tunnel behind us collapsed. I had to buy Peta time. I had to buy myself enough time to save her.

I lifted my spear over my head, let Spirit and Earth strengthen my muscles beyond anything I'd ever felt, and drove the blade down between two of Scar's vertebrae. He dropped under me, paralyzed, but not dead. I yanked my spear out, slid off him and ran to his mouth.

Bella was tugging at me and I pushed her back. I dropped my spear and grabbed Scar's mouth to yank it open. "PETA!" Nothing. "Don't make me come in there, cat." My voice wavered, the false anger barely keeping me from losing my mind. Shaking, I held his jaws open, holding the weight of them above me. I would hold them as long as I had to. "Bella, can you see her?"

Her hands were on my arms. "Lark, she leapt into his mouth to save you. We have to go. She is dead."

I shifted my hands so I could stand on his bottom jaw and hold the top up with both hands. "Peta, please."

Bella tugged at me, and my heart tugged in the other direction. Taking a deep breath, I forced myself to concentrate on the bond between Peta and me. I would know if she was gone. I would.

A tiny flicker of gray and white at the back of his mouth caught my eye at the same time I felt her heartbeat inside my own body. "She's alive. Bella, please." I looked over at my sister, and goddess love her, she never hesitated.

Bella dropped to her knees and crawled inside Scar's mouth to the back. She scooped up Peta and crawled back out, covered in slime. And blood. I dropped Scar's mouth and held my hands out. Bella gave Peta over to me. "Lark, she's hurt but alive. I'm not sure I can say the same for us if we don't get the hell out of here. The Firewyrms are almost through the rock."

Scar moaned. "The small pathway to the left. It will take you to the throne room. The one you used before. Do not worry about me. I will heal."

I put a hand on his nose as we passed, unable to hate him. Manipulation, how far had it gone in my world? Was everyone I'd known touched by Spirit?

We slid into the small tunnel as the other Firewyrms arrived. Bella scooted ahead of me and I clutched Peta to my chest, feeling her life flickering unsteadily. "Bella, we have to stop. I have to heal her."

I sat up, hunched over in the narrow tunnel. The dim light that came from the end we'd entered was not enough to see Peta's injuries. Not that I needed to. I held her tightly to me and let my energy flow into her body, using the bond between us first. She let out a pitiful mew, raised her head and then let it lower again.

Gathering Spirit, I wove the element through her body, feeling the wounds in her belly where Scar's teeth had pierced. Carefully I put her back together until the injuries were nothing but a faint memory. I slumped where I was, exhausted. Bella sat beside me. "Lark, you can't face Fiametta like this."

"We can't stay here," I pointed out.

Peta slept, snoring softly. I clutched her to my chest, finally allowing myself to see how close I'd come to losing her for real. Her heartbeat had slowed to the point that I knew it only had a few beats left in it.

"Too close," I whispered.

Bella put her head against mine. "Her job is to protect you."

"And if she breaks me by dying? That won't protect me, it will destroy me completely." The words slipped out of me before I could catch them.

Bella let out a sigh. "You would survive, Lark. You always do."

I wasn't so sure she was right. Peta was a part of my soul, and the thought of losing her was beyond anything I'd ever experienced. I'd killed my own father and felt less pain. I'd lost my mother and little brother and slowly the grief had faded.

I wasn't so sure the same could be said if Peta died. I suspected I would go mad with grief if I lost her.

I rubbed a hand over my face, thinking. So much for taking the stones back with ease. "How the hell are we going to do this?" I didn't ask because I thought she would have an answer. My question was for myself.

Bella was silent a moment. "I could go to Flint. He would listen to me. He might even be able to get the ring from his mother."

I hated to put this on her, but if we could avoid another confrontation, then I would take that chance. I opened my vest and tucked Peta inside. She snuggled against my skin, but otherwise didn't stir. "Let's try, if you think he would help you."

She scooted ahead of me, her voice echoing back. "I'm pregnant with his child, he'd better help me."

Shock rocked me back and for a moment I couldn't move. Then I was shooting forward. I grabbed her foot. "Excuse me? When the hell were you going to tell me you were pregnant? And I let you come with me on this journey and you've been in danger the whole time! I never would have allowed you to come—"

"I know." She jerked her foot from my hand. "That's why I didn't tell you. I want to help, I need to help. And this baby needs to have a world that will allow for half-breeds to live. I don't know that he or she will be strong like River. Or you. I don't want this baby to end up a slave in the Deep." She led the way in the pitch black, her voice echoing back to me. "You already are protecting me, Lark. I trust you to keep us both safe."

Us. I closed my eyes and crawled after her. "Bella, you should have told me."

"I wasn't certain when we left the Rim. I felt the baby kick when we landed on the mountain."

Of course the baby would recognize its home. My heart lurched for Bella. Half-breeds were drawn more strongly to one side of their heritage. Cactus was drawn to the Rim and his Terraling side. River was drawn to the Rim too, instead of the Deep.

But if the baby Bella carried reacted here at the Pit, there was a good chance he or she would be drawn to the fire in their blood.

Ahead of us, light trickled in along with the sound of voices. Bella slowed and I caught up to her. The tunnel tightened until it touched my back and belly at the same time. Peta let out a muffled mew and I touched her head. "Shh. Go back to sleep, lazy cat."

Bella slid out of the tunnel while I was distracted. She stepped around the huge statues that blocked the view of the tunnel.

"Flint," she whispered.

A gasp and the sound of lips on lips. "Bella, love, how

did you get in here? Does my mother know you're here?" His voice had a lovely deep timbre; even I could see how she'd be seduced by it.

"Please, your mother can't know I'm here."

The sound of shuffling cloth, as if he'd pulled her tightly against him. I hoped for her sake he did love her. That he wasn't using her. Call me cynical, but after dealing with Cactus, I wasn't so keen on Salamanders and their professed love.

I shimmied close to the edge of the tunnel and slid out. Crouching behind the statue, I waited.

Bella cleared her throat. "My sister helped me get in. We need your help, though."

"Your sister? Briar is here?"

That was my cue. I stood and stepped around the golden statue of Fiametta. "No, the trouble-making sister."

Flint's eyes widened, but he caught himself quickly. "Larkspur. I'd say welcome, but your name is somewhat synonymous with chaos and destruction."

I smiled, but it wasn't a nice smile. "Your mother, how is she?"

He shook his head. "Psychotic. But that's why you're here, isn't it? To remove her from the throne?"

Apparently that was what I was remembered for as much as the trouble I caused. Removing unsuitable rulers from their thrones. I didn't like that association any more than I liked being associated with destroying things.

I cleared my throat. "Something like that. We need to get the ruby off her first."

I hadn't even finished speaking when he started to shake his head. "It'll never happen. She's worn that ruby from the day you gave it to her and every day she's become increasingly unstable. And increasingly paranoid."

I narrowed my eyes. "You know what the ruby is?"

He shrugged. "Doesn't take a genius to figure out that it holds power. I added things together and it is the only thing that changed after you left. That, and the last person who asked to see the stone was beheaded."

The three of us stood silent for a moment.

"Does she sleep?" Bella asked.

He wrapped an arm around her shoulder, his deep gold eyes never leaving her face. He brushed a stray curl back from her cheek with his other hand as he smiled at her. Damn, it did look like love. Then again, looks could be deceiving.

"When she does she has the Firewyrms who are left guard her bedchamber. She trusts no one else."

I waved a hand at the doors. "Maybe standing out front of your mother's throne room as we discuss her is a bit like tempting fate?" I pointed out. "Is there a better place to talk?"

He shook his head and his eyes flicked away from me. Like he couldn't hold my gaze. "There is no safe place to talk. Your friend Cactus found that out the hard way."

A sudden lurch in my gut slowed my response. "What do you mean?"

Flint tightened his hold on Bella. "I can't protect you both. You understand that? Without Fiametta wearing the ring, I could face my mother. I am strong enough to beat her."

"That's not what I've heard." The words popped out of me before I could catch them. Peta snickered softly against me, then burrowed down again.

He didn't snap at me, though, only smiled. "I let people believe I am weak. Don't you find it leaves them unsuspecting when you finally show your true colors, Destroyer?"

I tipped my head. "Though that is true, I didn't plan it that way, and that is the difference between you and me."

He smiled. "Yet still, it has worked in my favor and yours. I could have trumped her before, but now there is no way. She is too tightly bound to the volcano and has threatened to let it loose on us."

"You'd survive," I pointed out.

"For how long?" Both his eyebrows went up. "Even the Firewyrms need to breathe. I'm talking about her filling the mountain with lava and destroying her own people. For no reason other than she chooses to."

I didn't want to like Flint, but I could see his mind at least was a match for Bella's and that softened me a little.

"Then I will face her if I must. You keep Bella safe, we are in agreement on that." I slipped Peta out of my vest and she blinked one green eye at me.

"Lark—"

"No, I will worry about you too much. And you are no good to me in the shape you are in."

Bella took her and cradled her. Peta didn't squirm, but her eyes never left mine. "Do not die on me, Lark."

"I don't plan on it."

Flint straightened. "You have a plan?"

I stared at the throne room behind us. "Get your family out, Flint. And get them out fast."

From the leather pouch at my side I sifted through the stones. The five fake ones I pushed to the side, and I pulled out the two real rings I'd collected so far. There was something about them that was more vibrant than the fake ones. I couldn't put my finger on it, more like a glimmer of the possibility that lay within them. I wondered if it was just me that saw it, or if my connection to Spirit allowed me to see beneath the surface.

The real emerald and sapphire blinked up at me, beckoning. Did I dare use them, hoping I would not be pulled under the spell of their creator?

Did I dare face Fiametta in all her rage and madness without them?

CHAPTER 15

"She is in the lower levels with everyone." Flint broke my concentration as I stared at the stones.

I clenched my hand around the emerald and sapphire. "Bella, I need a piece of your skirt."

"Really?" Flint stared hard at me. "You need to change clothes before you see Fiametta?"

"No." I bent to one knee and grabbed the bottom edge of Bella's full skirt. "I need to prepare myself before we deal with her." I cut off a strip and laid it on the ground. I poured out the fake stones onto the material and wrapped them tightly. If I needed to grab the real ones, the last thing I needed was to scramble and waste time sifting through the fakes. I tucked the bundle into my leather pouch and then set the real stones on top.

"Now I am ready."

Flint raised an eyebrow but didn't question my actions further. "There is no way to get my people out without alerting her. And you need someone to lead you in and out." He took Bella's hand and strode ahead. "I think the best way would be to get Bella out, and you and I will face my mother. I won't risk Bella being hurt."

My lips twitched. "Bella, I approve. And you should probably tell him."

She swung back to me, her mouth an *O*, her eyes filling with tears. I blamed those on the hormones.

Flint didn't slow, typical man didn't even seem to hear me, or get the undertones of my words. "We have to hurry. Tell me on the way," he said.

I laughed. "Oh, I think this might slow you down."

Bella shook her head, and I knew what she was wondering. Why now? Why tell him she was pregnant now of all times? And then I saw the understanding sweep over her face.

There was a chance he would not survive what was coming. It was why we wanted her moved to safety. My mistake was thinking it would help her say her piece and move to safety.

"No, I'm coming with you." She slid to a stop. "I am coming with you. I am queen of the Rim, and I will not run from a battle."

"Peta cannot come with us, she's still healing," I pointed out.

"Then we will put her outside and Shazer can pick her up."

Worm shit. "Bella, there is no time to argue—"

"Which is why you should stop trying to protect me. I'm not an invalid," she snapped.

I put a hand on her shoulder and physically dragged her toward the entrance, which I could see now glimmering in the darkness. The black obsidian rock shined in the flickering torchlight. "It's my job to protect you. You are my sister and my queen. You are the important one in our family. My life for yours. Always."

Flint nodded. "Listen to her, my love. Being queen does not mean you must always fight. Your sister is doing her job. You must do yours. My people will need to be organized as I send them out."

He kissed her softly then and all her resistance faded. Peta raised a sleepy eyebrow at me. "You going to kiss me goodbye?"

I snorted a laugh, and rubbed one of her ears. "No, your breath smells like fish."

Flint opened the door, and it was only then I realized there were no guards. We probably could have walked right in the front entrance without being stopped. Bella stepped into the forest of ever-blooming cherry trees. The soft pink petals floated around her, some sticking in her hair. She raised a hand and we all took a step back.

The obsidian door slid closed and I turned to Flint. "Don't you dare hurt her."

He grinned. "I'm defying a world of rules, of expectations, just by being with her. The last thing I would do is hurt her."

"Good. Just so we're clear. I'll cut your balls off and dice them into a puree if you so much as make her cry."

His grin faded. "That I believe. Sister." He winked, and I saw the same charm Cactus had worked on me for so long. I only hoped Flint turned out better than Cactus in the end.

"Let's go."

Flint led the way, and I thought he would keep to himself.

"Do you know what she was going to tell me?" He glanced at me and I shook my head.

"I do, but it's not my place. Certainly not now." Because I didn't want him to turn around and run back to her. He was right, I needed a guide here in the Pit. The twists and turns of the labyrinthine place were the same as before. There was no way I'd find my way without help.

And after my run-in with Scar, I wasn't sure any of my old friends would be the ones I could go to. I slid to a stop as the realization hit me.

"What?" Flint stopped with me.

The people attacking me, the people causing problems were all those who'd helped me in the past. Whoever was controlling the stones knew me far better than I knew them.

"Nothing." I waved him off. "Keep going."

He gave me a look but said nothing more. "How do you want to do this?"

I swiped at my face, wiping the sweat from my eyes. "How well does she trust you? At all? Can you get close to her?"

"Closer than you," he said. "Maybe ten or fifteen feet."

I nodded. "I want you to do that. Get as close as you can and be ready to tackle her."

"And get the ring."

I nodded. "Toss it to me immediately. You can be controlled through it." The last thing I needed was for Flint to put the ring on and make it so I had to deal with him too.

"Lava piss, then I was right? I'd hoped . . ."

I nodded. "Yes. But if she's used the ring a lot, her mind will be chewed up. Just like Cassava." I hadn't meant to say that last bit.

He opened his mouth, but I beat him to it.

"Yes. She had a ring like the one your mother is wearing." A ring I'd buried in the bottom of Griffin's hut years ago. I swallowed hard, suddenly realizing I'd not checked to make sure it resided there still. Worm shit, I forgot to grab it before I left the Rim, but in the grief of having to end my father's life, it had slipped my mind.

One thing at a time. I would go back for the pink diamond at the end of the journey. There was no way Blackbird would find it.

We reached the end of the tunnel we were in and Flint held out his hand to stop me. He put a finger to his lips and peered around the edge. His whole body stiffened. I hurried to his side and looked out.

The main floor of the living area was a wide plateau, and in the center was a living oasis I'd created with Cactus's help. That had been my gift to Fiametta and the Salamanders before I'd left.

Where it had stood was a monstrous fire that licked the ceiling of the cavern, thick black smoke filling the room. The fire crackled and hummed, happily destroying every living thing in its path.

"She has everyone here," Flint said quietly. I put a hand on his arm.

"Where is her familiar?" Fiametta had had a black panther named Jag as her familiar the last time I'd been in the Pit. I'd hoped she would listen more to his advice, but it looked like he was being ignored once more.

"She killed him," Flint said, his voice flat.

Holy hell on fire, she was as lost as my father. I could not understand how either of them had the ability to kill their familiars. The thought of Peta dying had sent my mind into a state of sheer panic, but to be the one who'd killed her? What had that done to Fiametta when she realized she was the hand of death? I remembered all too clear my father's attempt to destroy the Spiral and the Rim.

There were more children than Flint who belonged to

Fiametta. I didn't want to ask, but I made myself spit the question out. "And your younger siblings?"

He shook his head and his eyes blurred. "She sent me to the Rim. She knew I was interested in Bella. When I came back they were buried . . . I should have been here, Lark. I could have stopped her."

"Why would she send you away?"

He squeezed his eyes shut and then opened them once more. "I have always led her to believe I am weak, uninterested in the throne. She has believed me all these years. The others openly spoke of being the ruler one day. It . . . saved me, even while it damned my brothers and sister. If I had known what she was about, I would have taken them with me and left them in the Rim, come back and faced her on my own."

I put a hand on his shoulder, feeling the loss of Bramley and understanding all too well the desire to protect your siblings—and failing.

"I doubt that. You would have died too and then where would your people be? You are here now. We can make this right. Or as right as is possible." Goddess, I hoped we could. "What are the chances we're going to make this happen without a full-on war? You know her mental state, if she killed her own familiar and children . . ."

He drew in a slow breath. "I think we will have to kill her. I don't see her backing down, or seeing any sense."

That was what I was afraid of. "And are you ready to lead your people if that happens?"

He nodded. "I am."

"And marry my sister, uniting two families?"

His eyes widened. "Pushy much?"

I tightened my hand on him. "For her? Yes."

He grinned. "Yes, I plan on it. She and I will change things."

I nodded. "Good enough for me. I want you to go to the other side of the plateau, get your mother's attention and keep it. I'm going to hit her from behind."

Flint clapped me on the back, turned and disappeared into the tunnel we'd just left. I crept out and onto the ledge. Shimmying down the rock face, I dropped to the main floor with a soft thud. No one looked back at me. So far so good.

Fiametta was yelling at someone, and though I couldn't hear the words, I knew it wasn't good. The tone was that deadly mixture of anger and calculation that only she had, of fire and ice that made you want to shiver and melt away at the same time.

I hurried along the curve of the room until I was as close as I could get without exposing myself. Crouching next to the edge of one of the living quarters, I peeked around, trying to get a look without being seen myself.

Fiametta strode back and forth in front of her people; I could only catch glimpses of her.

"Time and again, I've protected you, and what do I get for it? Suspicion, my own people plotting against me, my own son defying my commands!" Her deep red hair flew behind her, she strode so fast. "And then, a spy is sent, a spy that tried to use my love for him against me."

Worm shit, that had to be Cactus. The crowd in front of me shifted and for a split second I saw my childhood friend on the ground, a pool of blood around him, before the crowd closed again, hiding him from view. My heart clenched at the thought of him dying. No matter that we would never be a couple, I still cared for him. He was still my friend.

Fiametta spun suddenly and the crowd gasped. Whatever Flint was doing, this was my cue. I sprinted through the crush of bodies, pushing elementals out of my way as fast as I could. I broke through, and saw Cactus. There was nothing I could do for him if I didn't stop her. I leapt at Fiametta.

She spun at the last second and raised her hand to me. Brilliant red lines of power rippled up her arms and the blast caught me mid-air. I was flipped over backward, the front of my vest on fire.

I hit the ground, rolled and put the fire out. "Fiametta, you are going to kill your own family!"

She didn't answer me. Flint crept closer, but she seemed to sense him. She spun and flicked a hand at him. A pure rope of lava sprang from her hand and wrapped around his waist. If it tightened . . . he'd be cut in half.

I called up my connection to the earth and opened the ground under Fiametta, drawing her attention back to me. She snarled and dropped her son. I closed the ground around her feet and drew her further down into the stone until only her head was visible. The same trick I'd used on her the last time I'd been in the Pit.

Only this time, it didn't work the way I'd hoped. The lava and fire didn't stop. If anything, it ramped up to an even greater rate of death and destruction. The lava that cut through the plateau rose and swept toward me at an unnatural speed, heating the air to the point where breathing was a serious effort.

Flint and Cactus would be hit first, and I wasn't sure they'd survive the lava in their injured states, despite their bloodlines.

I didn't have time to consider the consequences, it was either act now or die as the lava closed in on me. I grabbed my leather pouch and pulled out the sapphire. Gripping it,

I tapped into the water available, the river that ran perpendicular to the lava flow.

Using all three powers open to me, I poured Spirit into Earth and Water, boosting what I could do with them. I opened the earth in a line in front of the oncoming lava. Diverting the river, I flooded the banks and drew it toward the burning oasis, putting the fire out.

Fiametta stared at me as she pulled herself from the stone inch by inch, dripping with sweat, and I realized how she'd done it. She'd melted the stone around her, softening it so she could free herself.

"You lying little bitch. You are taking the stones for yourself. You think you can rule our world? That isn't possible. None of it is possible, no matter what he says."

At the far edge of the plateau, four Firewyrms emerged from a sidewall entrance I'd not seen.

Flint groaned and pushed himself to his feet, one arm clutched around his middle. "Lark, you must end this now. They will kill us all if she gives the word."

Fiametta snapped her fingers as if his words had reminded her that she had that ability. The Firewyrms surged forward, teeth snapping, scales sparkling. The crowd didn't move, though, as if they were held by unseen bands.

"Run, you idiots!" I yelled, and the spell over them was broken. They scattered.

"The main door!" Flint commanded. They listened to him, and the Firewyrms seemed uncertain about whom to attack—the Salamanders, or me. The pause gave me a chance to stave them off.

I spun my spear out and sprinted toward Fiametta. Weaving Spirit and Earth together again, I used them to tear up the ground in front of the Firewyrms. There was no finesse needed here and my elements reveled in the lack of control. Chunks of rock and dirt exploded in a line, smashing into the big lizards. At another flick of my hand the ground rippled and threw them to the entranceway. I couldn't stop them completely, but I could buy some time.

Flames burst up at my feet, burning the side of my leg. I jumped to one side, rolled in the dirt, and up onto my feet again. But the flames did not slow. I spun and saw Fiametta through the fire, and another figure behind her.

I threw my spear, deliberately aiming to one side. Fiametta dodged the weapon easily and laughed.

"You are a failure, just like your friend." She motioned to the ground behind her. Only he wasn't on the ground.

From behind her, my spear was shoved through her back. She stiffened, a scream on her lips, but no sound came out.

Cactus caught her as she slumped. "I'm sorry, Fiametta. It had to be done."

"And so did this," she whispered. Her hands clutched his face and they lit on fire. He screamed, and I ran to them. I tackled Fiametta away from Cactus, slamming her against the hard-packed dirt, which jammed the spear in further. She laughed, blood flowing over her lips. I grabbed her hand and pulled the ring off.

Not that it would do us any good now.

Flint was at my side, tugging at me. "We have to go."

"She's dying."

He jerked me hard. "She's unleashed the lava."

I snapped my head up as the lava burst out of the seam in the earth I'd sucked it into. "Worm shit." I considered putting the ruby on.

This world is dying, child. Let it die. Let us start again, fresh and new.

The voice was the same as the one from the Deep. The

same voice from the Eyrie when the mountain had spoken to me, told me it was time to take it back from the Sylphs. A shiver rolled through me. I was not going to argue with something that felt as though it was every element in the world wrapped into one consciousness.

At the same time, I didn't agree with the voice. Not for a second was I going to just let this world die.

"Worse," Flint said, pulling me back to the present, "this is far worse than worm shit."

I stood, and pulled my spear from Fiametta's back. She continued to laugh.

"I've killed you all, and now I've done what he's been telling me to do."

I crouched beside her, tempting fate, but I had to know. "Who's been telling you what to do?"

Her blue eyes were wide, rimmed with white and suddenly afraid. "I can't tell you that, no not that."

"You can," I whispered, knowing this was it, the moment Talan would be outed in his games, his subterfuge. "You can tell me. He won't hear you. I promise."

Her hands gripped my forearms suddenly, with a force that pinned me down so we were nose to nose. She shook, the intensity of her grip not slipping an inch though I could feel her dying, could almost see the life slip from her. "He will kill us all if he is the chosen one. You can stop him, Lark. You must, you will save us, or you will destroy us, but both will save us." Her hands slipped from my arms, leaving perfect imprints of her fingers. She fell back, her head thumping the stone with a sickening thunk.

As if a signal were given, Fiametta's death rolled through the volcano in a ripple. Her body sank into the mountain and I took a step back, the slow-growing sinkhole around her body opening further.

"Lark, what are you doing?" Flint yelled.

"This isn't me. This is the mountain on its own." I glanced at the ground, as if it would give up its secrets. The hole spread farther and a blurp of lava spit up as Fiametta's body slid into the crevice. Gone.

As if she never existed.

I spun, grabbed Cactus from the ground, yanked him up across my shoulders, and broke into a sprint. He let out a low groan but otherwise kept his mouth shut. There was no time for niceties. Whatever was happening would swallow us all if we stood still.

Flint herded his people ahead of him, even as I saw the lines on his arms. He turned and tried to slow the lava, but it had a life of its own. "It's tied to her death somehow."

"Booby trap," Cactus mumbled.

I flicked a hand behind us and pulled the stone down. The mountain shuddered and rumbled. "Move it!" I could feel the lava splash against the stone, and begin to creep through the blockage.

The feel of the heat on the stone slowed my feet and I stopped where I was. My eyes fluttered closed as warmth spread along my skin, as though I were the stone and the lava was caressing me. Spirit flared through me and I rolled my head back; there, at the edge of my conscious was something I'd been searching for—

"Lark, run!" Cactus broke my concentration.

Shock and anger coursed through me. "Damn it, Cactus." I ran forward once more, wanting that feeling of warmth, of a connection to an element that wasn't my own.

"Sorry for keeping us alive," he muttered. He was right; if I'd stood there we both would have been swallowed up in the lava.

And I'd wanted it.

That should have scared me . . . and the worst part was that it didn't. I wanted to feel that heat coursing through me again.

No matter the cost.

CHAPTER 16

The obsidian doors were behind us and we were free of the Pit, but we had to keep moving. Lava flowed out of every crevice of the mountain in gulping spurts as though it wanted to eat us, the brilliant red against the green grass and trunks of the cherry trees not slowing even though it was far from the source. The crack and rumble of falling stone, the splash of boulders crashing as the mountain crumbled. It reminded me all too well of the Eyrie. I glanced back in time to see the top of the mountain sink from view, sucked down with a boom that felt as though thunder rocked the earth.

"Keep running!" I yelled. We were far from safety. With the mountain destroyed, the lava would flow for a long time. Whatever hold Fiametta had on the lava was keeping the Salamanders from even trying to control it.

Ten miles away, the group finally stopped, the lava left behind to devour whatever it wanted.

Flint kept a hand on Bella the whole way, I kept Cactus on my shoulders and Peta watched me from Bella's arms.

I wanted to ask her about what I'd felt inside the mountain. The sensation of the lava against my skin, hot but not hurting me. As if I were a Salamander. But that wasn't possible. The ruby lay inside my leather pouch, and even if I'd been wearing it, there was no way the lava wouldn't have swallowed me whole. It was as unnatural to the Salamanders as it was to me.

Shazer landed ahead of us. "What the hell did you do?"

I slid Cactus from my shoulders and took a deep breath. "I didn't. Not this time."

It was only then I realized that none of the Firewyrms had escaped with us. I closed my eyes and went to my knees, the cool grass little comfort against the thoughts that raged in my head. Had they been condemned to death along with Fiametta?

And worse, did I care?

I swallowed hard and opened my eyes. "Bella, you're okay?"

She nodded. "You got what you came for?"

I touched my leather pouch. "Yes. I don't want you to come with me now. Go home to the Rim."

Her eyes narrowed. "You will not order me around. I am your queen."

I rolled my eyes. "And you're pregnant."

Flint went rather still next to her. "You're pregnant."

Bella flushed. "I only just found out."

He pulled her into his arms and the crowd tightened around them, reaching out to touch them both. I looked for familiar faces in the crowd of Salamanders. For Brand and his wife Smoke. For their three boys, Stryker, Tinder and Cano. But they weren't there.

"The battle with Orion." Peta trotted across the grass to me. "All five of them were lost in the battle."

I gave her a sharp nod of acknowledgment but could barely swallow past the guilt and grief that swelled. Once more I had to consider that Talan may have been right. What if I'd not needed to bring the four families into the battle? If I'd not done that, my friends would still be alive.

"Do not doubt your choices now," Peta said. "Whatever has you doing that is wrong. The world would not have survived without your help. Without the elementals stepping up to help the world. And it was their choice, Lark. You know that. Why are you doubting yourself now?"

"Talan . . . he said things about the battle."

She sucked in a sharp breath.

I looked her right in the eye. "I think I hate him, Peta."

Her shoulders slumped. "I know."

Not that she hated him too, but she knew I hated him. Mother goddess help me if I lost her to him.

Someone tugged at the back of my belt. "I know you all are busy, but do you think you could help me out?"

I turned to Cactus. His injuries were bad, but mostly superficial. I ran a hand over his head. The imprints where Fiametta's hands had gripped him were healing already. He'd have some scarring, from the burns, but they would fade with time. Even the injury that had caused all the blood was smaller than I'd thought. A gash at the back of his head that was only an inch long and already had slowed.

"You'll be fine." I let go of him and stood, already thinking about the Eyrie.

Cactus grabbed my leg. "Lark, please. Heal me. I'm in pain."

I blinked several times, unsure that I'd heard him right.

"It costs me to heal, Cactus. A piece of my soul, maybe more each time. You'll have some scars, but you'll be fine."

His green eyes closed. "Please, Lark. The pain is . . . intense."

I went back to my knees and put my hands on his cheeks. "I'm sorry you're in pain, but you will live and heal just fine on your own. Suck it up, buttercup."

His eyes flew open, all but crackling with anger. "I never thought I'd see the day you'd turn away from helping someone. Especially not someone you love."

"Loved," Peta said. "Past tense."

His hand shot out for her, red lines of power curling to his fingers, the intent all over him.

That he would even dare was the last drop in an overflowing bucket of no more patience.

I grabbed his hand and twisted it backward, the snap of bone clear as a bell in the still air. "Don't ever try to hurt her again, Cactus. I will choose her every time. Do you understand?"

His jaw dropped, but I didn't let go of the arm I'd broken. "Do you understand?"

"Yes." He whispered the word and I let him go.

Standing, I turned back to the crowd. Flint began a slow clap. "To defend a familiar like that. Brilliant, Lark, it's the way it should be done."

I held a hand out for Peta and she leapt into my arms. "You wouldn't really kill him over me, would you?" She blinked up at me.

I touched a hand to her back. "Yes. I would."

Her eyes widened farther, and through the bond I felt her surprise.

Flint smiled. "Just to be clear, I've always liked Peta."

I stepped away from Cactus and headed to where Shazer

waited. "Flint, I doubt that very much. As long as you treat her well now, that's all that matters."

"You'd doubt me?"

I turned and glanced back at him. "The charm of a Salamander is legendary. We all know it. I won't be charmed, Flint. I will take you at face value. End of story."

His smile slipped and he gave me a slow bow from his waist. "So between you and me, nothing but truth."

"Between you and me, nothing but truth. No matter how hard." I didn't bow back.

His grin grew. "You and I are going to be good friends, sister. I look forward to years of arguing with you."

I burst out laughing, caught off guard by his words. Bella smiled and lifted a hand, which caught everyone's attention.

"As queen of the Rim, I welcome all Salamanders to our home as a place to recoup and wait for your home to be safe once more."

Flint nodded. "Thank you. We will take you up on your offer."

The crowd shifted, looking from one to another. As if they weren't sure if they could follow Flint without a trial by fire. The way they chose their leader was sheer strength. Then again, he'd fought Fiametta and she'd been the one to fall.

They would soon see he was strong enough. Or maybe they'd seen enough in the cavern. I shook my head; what did it matter to me who ruled the Salamanders?

Worm shit, I did not want to be a meddler. A tiny voice I recognized as my own piped up.

Too late, idiot.

Bella tipped her head to one side. "We are family, even though we are sustained by different elements. If we do not stand with each other, who will?"

The Salamanders murmured their agreement. Bella and Flint got the people organized, setting them off in groups, sending those who could travel the easiest and fastest ahead of the rest.

None of it really mattered to me; I had a job to do. And Ash to find. His name tightened in my belly. How many days since I'd thought of him? In all the chaos and fighting, I'd barely had time to consider how much closer I was to the mother goddess helping me.

I reached Shazer and ran a hand over his neck. He head-butted me in the belly lightly.

"Is your sister coming with us?"

"It is her choice," I said. "She's my queen; I can't stop her."

Footsteps on the grass turned me around. I expected Bella. What I got was an agitated and fired-up Cactus.

"You seriously are going to just leave me here?" he spluttered. "Like I'm nothing to you?"

I leaned my head against the Pegasus. "I would rather bed Shazer at this point than you, Cactus. At least I know I can trust him not to try to manipulate me."

Shazer snorted. "Don't tempt me, you have a lovely ass."

I rolled my eyes and slapped a hand against his hide. "Don't try to help."

Cactus stared at me, his hair matted with blood, his face burned and his eyes as angry as I'd ever seen them. A sudden thought rolled through my head. His behavior was just off enough to make me think he was being an ass. But what if he had been affected too? Like Scar, Finley, and the others? I reached out to take his hand and he pulled me toward him.

I pushed a pulse of Spirit through him, looking for something that controlled him other than his own thoughts.

Nothing resided in him.

Everything he was doing was just Cactus being a prick. I pulled back, sadder than I'd been in a long time. "Cactus, we are friends, but you are putting even that to the test."

"I'm the one putting it to the test? You ask me to come to the Pit, I get injured trying to help you, and you won't even heal me? What kind of friend is that?" He was yelling and people were looking. If he thought causing a scene was going to bother me, he had another think thing coming.

I put a hand to his chest and shoved, sending him back a good ten feet. "What kind of friend tries to manipulate someone he says he loves? What kind of friend is okay with her losing a *piece of her soul* for the sake of his vanity? Piss the hell off, Cactus, and stay out of my life. Do you understand? Because the next time you come at me, I won't hold back. You tried to hurt Peta. You tried to manipulate me time and again. I change my mind. We are not friends. I do not want you in my life. Got it, Prick?"

He pushed himself up, and brushed his hands over his legs. "Yeah. I got it. Bitch." He walked away, without a single look back.

"Finally," Peta muttered.

I fought the bitter laugh that teased at my mouth. Peta was right. *Finally* was the only word that fit. After all this time, Cactus finally understood that we were done. We could have been friends, but he'd broken that too when he'd tried to hurt her.

Like the idiot he was, he thought I'd forget all he'd done because he batted his green eyes at me.

Shazer yawned. "You have a way with men, you know that?"

"You have no idea," I muttered, thinking of Coal. And

suddenly afraid that maybe I was the asshole. What would happen when Ash and I were together again? Would I chase him off too?

"Relax. I would tell you if it was your fault," Peta said, obviously picking up on my train of thought.

Shazer nodded. "Agreed. He's a giant dick. You were right to send him away."

I smiled, but the edges of it fell. "Right. Let's get going. There is no way the Eyrie won't be waiting on us. I'd hate to disappoint them."

I mounted up on Shazer's back and tightened my legs around his sides, urging him forward.

He paused. "What about Bella?"

I spotted her a good distance away. "She was with me to play the diplomat. To help things go smoothly. You think the Eyrie will go any smoother than the Deep or the Pit?"

He shook his head. "No, but she's going to be pissed when she realizes you're gone without her."

I urged him forward again and he started his wind-up gallop. Bella spun as the sound of his hooves on the earth filled the air.

"Larkspur!"

I lifted a hand to her. "Be safe, Bella."

Shazer leapt into the air, and I pointed a finger at Flint. He saluted me, and I knew for better or worse, he was a part of our family. Maybe he always had been. I shook my head at the thoughts swirling through it.

Peta slid down my shoulder to sit in front of me, her paws resting on Shazer's neck. "Three of the five stones collected. Is the final stone where you left it?"

Shazer's ears perked up. "You had a stone already?"

"The pink diamond. But I hid it away."

"Smart." He bobbed his head as he angled his wings to

take advantage of a current of air. "Even though you know they're addictive, they would still begin to work on you."

Peta's tail twitched almost spasmodically. "Lark isn't stupid. She's been careful with the stones right from the beginning. Unlike these other fools who wear them as if they aren't capable of ruling otherwise."

I placed a hand on her. "Not their fault, either. Not really. None of us understood what the stones were truly for until it was too late."

And that was the crux of it. In that, what Talan had said was right: it was my fault all this had happened. I'd given the stones to the leaders of the four families without any thought to there being a consequence. I shook my head as the guilt piled on my shoulders.

"Where is Blackbird in all this? We have seen neither hide nor hair of him, though he is hunting the same stones," Peta asked suddenly, breaking my line of thought.

I rubbed a hand on one thigh. "I'm hoping he is behind us somewhere, the Rim or the Deep, looking and not realizing the stone is gone."

Peta yawned, her tiny jaw cracking wide. "Wishful thinking. What are you really thinking?"

The thing I'd not been able to dismiss rose out of my mouth. "That he's waiting for me to gather all five stones and then take them from me. A single fight he knows he will win, rather than tiring himself out on four different rulers."

"Exactly," she whispered. "That was my thought exactly."

There was something that bothered me, though. "There are still things that don't fit."

"Like what?" Shazer threw the question back.

"Let's go through this logically," I said. "Bella fought me, and then our father lost what was left of his mind. From there, we went to the Deep where Finley set an assassin on me, we fought her, and then two Sylphs attacked us. In the Pit, we faced Scar who was being manipulated and then Fiametta who, like my father, had lost her mind." I paused and replayed the events over and over in my head, and only two notes stood out. "Each time, there has been a personal connection when I faced a ruler. My father. Scar. Bella. Finley. Except for the Sylphs who showed up at the Deep. They were no one I knew. There was nothing personal about that attack. Which tells me . . ."

"You aren't dealing with a single enemy, but two." Shazer's words were clear in the high, crisp air.

Two enemies, neither of which I was entirely certain I knew. But I couldn't deny Shazer was right, as much as I wished he were wrong.

I nodded.

"Exactly."

CHAPTER 17

The Himalayan Mountains reared into the sky in front of us. I pressed a hand against Shazer's neck. "I think we should land away from the Eyrie and see if we can get a look at the situation before we make any decisions."

He gave me a quick nod and spiraled out of the clouds. Peta shivered against me, though I doubted it had to do with the air temperature.

"What is it?"

"This place was not good to us. To either of us, and I doubt this time will be any better. It makes my tail puff up."

I grimaced. I couldn't disagree with her. To say I'd left the Eyrie on bad terms last time was an understatement. I'd essentially killed their old queen, destroyed their mountain home, and walked away without any form of punishment. And Samara, the new queen, had been clear that if I dared show my face again, my life would be forfeit.

"Peta, did you come back here after I was banished?"

"No. It is the one place I didn't study. Their library was destroyed when you and Cassava fought, and I wasn't sure Samara's threat didn't apply to me as well." She sniffed. "I could have snuck in and they'd have never known. But like I said, there was nothing to look at. The library is gone."

Shazer swept down the last few feet to an open valley that was far enough away from where the Eyrie had been that I thought we'd be unnoticed. He dropped down the last bit, his wings tucked in tight to his sides, and did a double hop that bounced me off his back. I landed in a crouch, but on my feet, and Peta grinned from where she clung to him. "Reflexes like a cat; you're getting there."

A half smile turned my lips up as I stood. "How far are we from the Eyrie?"

Peta ran up Shazer's neck, stopped on his head and lifted onto her back legs, peering toward the mountain. Not that standing on two feet would give her a better vantage point. Like a meerkat investigating the lay of the land for danger, she swayed and bobbed, but remained upright as she scanned the area around us. I raised my eyebrows, surprised that Shazer held still for her to use him essentially as a step stool.

He grunted, as if he realized what was going on, and shook his head. She clung to him with her back feet, shocking me that she was still upright. "Hold still, hay bag."

"Hay bag? I just flew you two around the world the last few days. Show a little respect. Pussy."

She tightened her back claws in the top of his head. "The Eyrie is two valleys over. Assuming the Sylphs stayed in the same mountain."

"They'd have to," I said. "They are tied to it, as surely as the Undines are tied to the Deep. They would have had to rebuild in the same place to keep their people from going mad with homesickness."

"Take your stinking, dirty cat claws off me, you dirty stinking cat," Shazer drawled.

Peta flicked her tail. "Make me, oat eater."

I rolled my eyes and put a hand to the ground while they bickered like an old married couple. Without thought, I called on my connection to the earth. Would it buck and fight me? The power waiting for me there was thick with the same entity I'd felt before.

A sentient being that seemed to be the mountain itself. But that wasn't possible. Was it? The mother goddess was the mother goddess, there was no other being—

Illusions, Larkspur. Your world is an illusion that shall soon be shattered in a way you could not understand before now.

I froze where I was, as if I'd been covered in ice for a thousand years. I didn't dare move. "Who are you? You've spoken to me in the Deep and the Pit, as well as twice here."

Peta meowed at me. "Who are you talking to?"

I didn't answer her. "Tell me who you are."

The presence shifted and rolled, tugging at me with the strength of the world behind it. *We are the ones from which your power comes. We are the beginning. And we will be the end.*

I swallowed hard. "Are you helping me?"

Peta crept to my side and crawled into my lap, "Lark, *who are you* talking—"

Yes, I was there in the Pit. You fight a battle that no one sees yet, Lark. The one who calls herself the mother goddess is not to be trusted.

Peta's jaw dropped. "Sweet savory catnip, you aren't talking to yourself, are you?"

The voice chuckled softly. *Peta, we see you. Your ties to Lark are deeper than any familiar. Your souls are entwined as they were meant to be.*

Peta clenched her paws and her tiny claws dug into my vest. "You are the voice I hear when I sleep."

I am. Be strong, little cat, and do not let the fear of losing Lark overtake you; you will never be without her again. There was a pause and in that moment, worry slipped off Peta. Through the bond, I felt her relax. I hadn't even known she was so afraid, and yet now that it was gone I could easily see the way she stood a little straighter, her eyes shining brighter.

Lark's power has woken us from a long sleep, one that buried us to keep us silent. And now we will guide you both as best we can.

We. I thought there was a feeling of more than one entity. Male and female.

Yes. We represent all.

"The Eyrie, I have to retrieve the final stone." I paused. "Do you have . . . advice?"

The stones are needed, but not for what you believe. A shudder rolled through the mountain and the voice fell silent.

I waited for several minutes, on the off chance they would say anything more. Finally I lifted my hands from the ground. "Well, that was . . . interesting."

Peta nodded and we both looked at Shazer, whose eyes were wide as saucers.

"Who the hell were you two talking to?"

I shrugged. "Don't really know."

He flipped his muzzle at me. "Take a guess."

"The mountain, I think."

Peta nodded. "Yes, that's as close a guess as any."

His eyelids fluttered. "If you both hadn't heard the voice,

I'd have said Lark was losing her marbles. As it is, any good news from the . . . mountain?"

I laughed at his careful wording. "Just that the stones are needed, but not for what I think."

"That doesn't help us get into the Eyrie without being struck down by lightning, does it?" he pointed out.

"No, but I have an idea." I smiled at him. "Think you could do a loop over the Eyrie and get some idea of the layout?"

He snorted and stomped a foot. "So just *I* get the lightning?"

"I don't think they will strike you. Not without me on your back."

He rolled his eyes. "The words, *I don't think*, are not exactly reassuring."

"Best I've got. I'm not going to lie to you." I stood. "If you don't want to do it, I understand."

He grunted, spun and galloped away, leaping into the air at the edge of the clearing. Peta sat beside me. "He's as prideful as any Sylph."

"Yeah, but it works in my favor from time to time." I walked to the edge of the clearing, my eyes going to the sky every few steps. I couldn't see him, and I hoped he would be okay.

"He's smarter than he looks." Peta trotted ahead of me.

I changed the subject. "What, or who, do you think that was? The mountain, yes, but under that . . . what the hell are we dealing with here, Peta?"

She jumped onto a downed log, and sat. "Powerful, we know that much. Tied to at least two mountains. And your power woke them up. But when?"

I thought back to the times I'd used everything I had. "When I destroyed the Eyrie, that was when I heard the voice the first time. Again in the Deep, and then in the Pit when I was fighting with Fiametta and the mountain was collapsing." And one other time that I hadn't thought of in years.

"I see your face. There is more, tell me."

"When I faced the shadow walker, during my banishment. I destroyed a fair bit of real estate and I felt the presence. It was distinctly male then, but there were no words, just raw power."

Peta closed her eyes, a frown on her cat lips. I sat beside her and scratched the back of her neck. She leaned into me and I waited on her to speak.

"There were things I read in the libraries, things that didn't make sense, but if what you are saying is true, perhaps . . ."

"Do you mean like the notes in the Deep? Did you actually get a chance to read them?" I asked.

Her eyes flew open. "Shit clumping kitty litter, I forgot about those! Yes, I did read them. They actually . . . they actually make what we are seeing here make more sense."

"And?"

Her face twisted like she'd eaten something sour.

"Peta, how bad could it be?"

"Well, it just—"

I stopped scratching her neck. "Spit it out."

She took a breath and then spoke faster than I'd ever heard her. "Basically, the papers said there was an elemental who caused all sorts of problems thousands of years ago. Chaos and trouble followed this elemental everywhere. And he or she, there was never a gender given, didn't care. They reveled in it, and as they grew in strength, he or she started to lay things out. Made the stones. Created monsters. Divided the families as they are now."

I leaned back on the log. "And this elemental is dead?"

Peta shook her head. "I don't know. It didn't say. If they weren't dead, they would be the oldest living elemental out there. Which falls into line with what Shazer has said about his creator."

My thoughts went to Talan. Peta didn't know him the way she thought she did.

I glanced at her and she was still frowning. "Okay, that's obviously not the worst of it, so what else did it say?"

Her eyes flicked to mine and away. "The elemental was the most powerful the world had ever seen. A half-breed."

A chill swept through me and I already knew the answer, but I needed to hear it from her. "What was he?"

"He or she was a Terraling Spirit walker. Just like you."

Just like me. One of the Tracker's more colorful phrases rolled off my tongue before I could catch it.

"Fan-fucking-tastic."

Peta's eyes popped open. "Lark, you never—"

"Sorry, slipped out. Too much time with Rylee." I opened my mouth to ask her if there was anything else pertinent. Any clue to what this elemental, who was just like me, might have done.

The rumble of thunder brought my head up. The sky darkened at a rate that could only mean one thing.

Shazer had been spotted. I ran to the center of the clearing to get a better look. Against the dark clouds, his white hide glimmered and shined.

"Get down here!" I yelled. He dropped like a stone as lightning snapped and cracked around him. A bolt landed at my feet, throwing me backward. I hit the ground and rolled, breathing hard. Peta shifted, and I held a hand out. "You can't stop lightning. We have to dodge it." The plan

I'd had was thrown out and a new one grew at a rapid pace. "Let them capture us."

"What?"

"They'll take us to Samara for judgment."

"Oh, goddess, this will turn all my black spots gray."

I grinned at her. "Probably."

Shazer landed, and I flapped my hands at him as he drew close. "Stay back, I'm going to let them capture me."

He shook his head. "Bad idea."

"Only idea." I shoved at him and he let me push him away as another bolt hit the ground. I opened myself to Spirit and Earth and wove them together, deliberately using them as one. They blended perfectly and didn't fight me.

Understanding hit me and I stood there like a fool. A bolt of lightning slammed into the ground on my left, waking me. Balance, this was what Talan had meant. Instead of using the elements always separately, I should be using them together.

But how was that going to help me now? Above me, three Enders floated on the air currents, their white leathers and hair swirling around them as they shifted and moved. Three Sylphs, that was more than I could handle on my own when all three were trained as Enders.

I was so screwed if I didn't get them to 'capture' me and instead decided to just kill me and take Samara my body.

That would seriously derail my plans.

The one on the left, Lefty, dropped lower until he was only twenty feet over my head. He swung a long shimmering silver rod at me, the end tipped in a sharp barb, not unlike the tips of the tridents in the Deep.

"Take their air!" Peta yelled.

Powering my muscles with the strength of the earth, and thinking of Peta with the fireflies, I leapt into the air to meet him, twisting to dodge the barbed point. His eyes widened and he tried to avoid me but I crashed into him. I wrapped my hands around his neck and squeezed.

"Nighty night."

He scrabbled at me, all training gone. There was no way to make yourself breathe, even as a Sylph, when your windpipe was cut off. His fellow Enders swept in as we crashed to the ground. I landed on him, felt the electricity in the air, and rolled as the lightning bolt slammed home. The buzz dissipated over Lefty, and I shoved him off me.

Two Enders left.

And I only needed one to make this work. I sprinted toward the taller of the two Enders. His legs dangling a few inches lower than the first had. I leapt from the ground, and snagged one foot.

"What the hell? Is she a shifter?" yelled his friend. It was only then I realized I'd easily leapt thirty feet into the air. There would be time to think about that later. I hung from his foot and lifted my own legs to wrap around his waist. I squeezed with all I had, compressing his belly, blocking his lungs from taking in air. Peta was right, the best way to stop them was to take away their air. They didn't know how to deal with it.

We dropped to the ground as he passed out, and the final Ender floated forty feet above me. "What the hell are you?"

"I am the Destroyer." The words hung between us, and he blanched so that his face matched his white leathers. His lips curled.

"Then let us see you survive a kiss of lightning."

Lines of power whipped around his arms, faster than I could track. I grabbed hold of Spirit and Earth and wove them tightly around each other, driving them deep into the earth, anchoring me. I waited with my head bowed, fear racing along my spine. "Let me be right about this."

"Lark, run!" Peta screamed. I held a hand out to stop her as a bolt of lightning hit me square in the chest.

I didn't fight it, didn't try to send it away.

I held it to me, cradling it in the power. It snapped and sizzled along my body, sending every tiny hair on my skin into orbit. Slowly, I raised my head, and held up one hand. The lightning pooled in my palm, writhing and twisting in on itself. But what the hell did I do with it? It wouldn't hurt the Ender, it was his element.

Cactus had been the protector of the Pit because he'd been able to weave stones into the flames he'd created, making a deadly mix even to those who carried fire as an element.

I lifted my other hand, and with it, called up three large stones. I pulled them to me and imbued them with the lightning bolt.

"Not possible, that is not possible," the Ender whispered, the wind bringing me the words as clearly as if he stood by my side.

"Anything is possible," I whispered back. With a flick of my fingers, I sent it flying at the Ender. He dodged the first two crackling stones but the third caught him in the side of the head.

It exploded in a shower of shrapnel and light, like the humans' fireworks. He dropped from the sky, hit the ground and was still.

I let go of the elements in me, but the feeling of the lightning hovered there still, making me shiver. Peta ran to the three downed Enders, sniffing them.

"All three are alive."

I walked toward them, not even breathing hard. As I

passed the first one, he groaned and his eyelids fluttered. I snapped my fingers over him. "Stay." Vines burst from the ground, holding him down.

Another groan, but he didn't otherwise try to fight me. The other two Enders I sunk deep into the mountain. Being buried alive sucked, but it wouldn't kill them. They'd get out eventually.

Maybe.

I shook my head and made myself slow down. The adrenaline was pumping fast enough that I knew I was spoiling for another fight. I crouched beside Lefty. "Do you have a name?"

"Ryk."

"Well, Ryk, you are going to help me get an audience with the queen."

"She'll kill you." He squinted up at me. "She hates you."

I shrugged. "Be that as it may, you are going to take me to her. As your captive."

He frowned, his white eyebrows dipping low over washed-out blue eyes. "Why?"

"You think she cares if *you* live or die? You think she gives a shit about one lowly Ender?"

He rolled his head from side to side. "She was an Ender. She trains with us still." Brave words, but the fear was heavy in them. He wasn't sure, and I needed to use that to my advantage.

Maybe every Terraling Spirit walker was an asshole. That would explain a lot.

I smiled, knowing it was far from nice. "Please. She's a queen. There's plenty more Enders where you came from. Now. You will help me."

I flicked my fingers at the vines, loosening them. He sat up and rubbed at the back of his neck. He was so new to being an Ender, I could almost see the moisture behind his ears.

"I could steal your air right now." His hand dropped to hover over a dagger at his waist.

I didn't waste time. I pounced on him, pinning him back to the ground even as I snagged the dagger from his waist and pressed it against his throat. "No, you couldn't."

"Your reflexes are improving, Lark," Peta said. "What changed?"

"I stopped doubting. I stopped hesitating." I blinked several times and realized the words were truer than even I knew until I said them.

Peta nodded, though, as if it made perfect sense. "About time."

I pulled the Ender to his feet, with the dagger still at his neck. "I think you understand me now."

"I won't take you to her. I won't." He straightened himself up. "You'll have to kill me."

Freedom is life to a Sylph.

The words gonged inside my head and I wasn't sure where I'd heard them. But they were true and I knew I could use them.

I sighed and held a hand out, softening the ground under him excruciatingly slowly, so that each inch he slipped further was felt on every part of his body. "No, I won't kill you. I'll just stuff you so deeply in the ground no one will ever find you."

His eyes popped open wide as he sank into the earth. He scrabbled at the edges, but I kept softening the ground, drawing him in inch by inch.

"One of your friends will help me." I walked away and motioned with two fingers over the living grave of the second Ender. His body slowly emerged. His leathers were no longer a gleaming white and dirt smeared his pale face.

Ryk sucked in a sharp breath and began to hyperventilate even as he scrabbled at the ground. So green at his job, he didn't realize that if he stole my air now, he'd stop sinking. But maybe then too, the panic was enough to keep his rational thoughts at bay.

I shook my head. What was Samara thinking, sending useless tits after me?

The question rolled around in my head, stopping me. She was smarter than that. Unless . . . unless she wanted me to make it all the way to her? That didn't make sense.

"Stop, I'll help you," Ryk panted, and I firmed the ground around him. He was up to his ribcage. "I'll help you."

I smiled and motioned upward with my right hand. He was pushed out of the ground like a dog spitting out a bone.

"Good boy."

I pushed his fellow Ender back into the earth. Shazer trotted up next to me and spoke quietly. "How did you know he would be afraid of being buried?"

"Claustrophobia, it's a problem amongst them," I said.

"How do you know that? They don't talk about that *ever*." His eyes narrowed, and I narrowed mine back at him.

"What do you know about Sylphs exactly?"

"More than you." He snorted and trotted to where Ryk dusted himself off. The young Ender paused and stared up at the Pegasus.

"Are you real then?"

Shazer snorted and butted his head against Ryk. "I'm real, you idiot. You aren't supposed to attack legendary creatures, you know."

Ryk closed his eyes. "I can't defy my queen or her consort. It was not my choice."

I shook my head. "Queens need to be defied if they are wrong."

He glanced at me. "You aren't going to hurt her, are you?"

"No. I'm here to make things better," I said.

His eyes lit up with hope. "Tell me you're getting rid of her consort."

That was an unusual request. "Why would I care who she's got in her bedroom?"

Ryk looked around like he expected someone to pop out and point a finger at him. "Because we all think he's controlling her."

I struggled to swallow around the sudden lump of certainty in my throat. "What is her consort's name?"

He took a breath and shook his head. "If I tell you, you might not remove him."

"Why wouldn't I do that?"

"Because he's your brother."

"aven is Samara's consort?" I spat the words out, horrified that they could be true. He was the only brother I had left alive. Unless Bramley was out there, waiting for me. I wasn't going there. Not yet.

Suddenly the strange attacks that didn't fit into the pattern I'd been seeing made sense. The Sylphs had been sent by Raven to kill me and take the stones I'd collected so far, rather than do it himself, the lazy bastard. But why then were all the Sylphs that had come at me weak, and easily dealt with? Could Samara be trying in her own way to keep me alive, by sending her youngest, most inexperienced Enders after me?

The thought had enough merit for me to hope it was the case.

I grabbed Ryk by the arm and dragged him close. "I will get rid of Raven, and keep your queen alive."

He grinned. "Then you need to let me tie your hands

together. I'll carry you over my shoulder; pretend you're unconscious. I'll drop you right at his feet."

I wanted to laugh at his eagerness, but I couldn't get over the fact that Raven had ingratiated himself into Samara's life. She knew who he was; she'd fought at my side against him.

"He has to be using Spirit on her," Peta said. "You know that."

I did know, but my mind revolted at the incredibly strong Sylph queen being sucked under his spell and controlled so completely.

Ryk turned me around and looped a thin rope over my wrists. "I won't tie it, so don't tug until you're ready to stand."

I nodded. "Drop me at his feet and back far away."

"Why?"

I didn't want to say because there was a good chance the Eyrie would be destroyed again. No, that was not the way to make sure Ryk continued to help me. "Because there will be a fight, and you need to stay out of it."

I turned and he lifted me over his shoulder with a grunt. "You Terralings are damn solid."

Peta took a swat at him. "Don't insult someone who could kill you with the snap of her fingers, airhead."

I grunted. "Peta, you and Shazer follow as if you're trying to catch up."

She bobbed her head and ran out of my line of sight. Ryk held onto me with one arm, and though I couldn't see the lines of power on him, we rose. The wind whipped in a snarling whirl, carrying us high above the first mountaintop and into the thin air.

"You killed the two Enders who came at you in the Deep, didn't you?" he asked, surprising me.

"One of them, yes. The other fell on his blade."

Ryk shook his head. "I tried to go on that mission."

"You wanted to kill me?" That was not a good sign when we were this far up. Mind you, Shazer could probably catch me, but he was no dragon with claws to reach out and snag me from the air.

"No, I wanted to be the one to bring you in. You're legendary here, you know. The Destroyer." He tightened his grip on me. "We're getting close."

"How old were you when I demolished the Eyrie?"

"I wasn't born yet."

I crunched my eyes shut. A baby indeed. He'd not have even seen his thirtieth year. Younger than I was at the time I'd destroyed the Eyrie.

"My queen," he called out as we hovered. I struggled not to react, but to keep my body still. "I bring you the Destroyer. My comrades were sunk deep into the earth, but I survived."

The sound of clapping and cheering rose into the air around us, and I dared to peek with one eye. The Eyrie was no longer high in the mountains, but deep in the valley I'd created. From the glimpses I could see, the layout was similar, with pillars, and open to the sky rooms.

"Bring her to me, Ender Ryk," Samara called. "I want to see her face before I kill her."

Worm shit, I was hoping I could talk her out of that part. "Remember, drop me and back the hell up."

"Please don't kill her. She is a good queen." Ryk gave me a squeeze and we dropped from the sky like a stone. He landed and threw me forward. I kept my eyes closed and let myself go boneless. I hit the solid stone floor and bounced, rolling several times before I came to rest with my hands under my back and my face to one side. Through narrowed eyes, I took in what I could. The crowd of Sylphs, rimmed with Enders, filled the small section I could see. Samara had not wasted time building their ranks.

"How is it, Ender Ryk, that you, the greenest of my Enders, managed to stop her, the one who decimated our mountain?" Samara didn't sound like herself. Her voice had a strange wispy tone as though she was out of breath while being angry.

"She attacked Aryl and Vista. She turned her back on me and I was able to take her down."

"Yet, she still took out Aryl and Vista? You weren't able to save them too?" Samara crooned the question.

A soft laugh rolled through the air, the laugh of someone I knew all too well. "My sister is playing possum, my love."

Worm shit. I jerked my hands, breaking the loose tie Ryk had done. I rolled to my knees and faced Samara.

I barely glanced at her, my eyes instead going to the man at her side. Raven's black hair was slicked back, and his blue eyes were as bright as ever. Full of laughter.

Or maybe that was madness.

"Sister, sister. Did you come to congratulate us?" Raven tucked his hands behind his back. As though we were on good terms.

I frowned as I slowly stood. "Congratulate you on manipulating a queen and making her your whore?"

The crowd sucked in a collective breath, and Samara's Enders began a low rumble.

I continued. "Congratulate you on hiding your true motives yet again as you attach yourself to a powerhouse?" I put my hands on my hips. "You were always a coward, Raven. I should have seen it sooner." He had to have the smoky diamond already, which meant he would be even more dangerous than before.

His eyes didn't narrow, didn't tighten with anger. "You don't understand, Lark. We are not so different, you and I. I've been pushing you, trying to get you to see what has to be done. To train you."

I burst out laughing. I couldn't catch the sound before it escaped me. I bent over, I laughed so hard. Sucking in a deep breath, I finally calmed myself, though I couldn't keep the smile off my lips. "You were training me when you sent Enders to try and kill me in the Deep?"

"Yes."

One attack accounted for.

"And when you manipulated Scar to attack me?"

"Yes."

"And when Father attacked the Rim?" Goddess, let that not have been—

"Yes, then too. I knew you wouldn't actually be killed. You're too strong for that. I've been trying to help you. *He* asked me to."

"Father asked you to?" I was confused. Why would Father have asked Raven to help me?

Raven shook his head. "No, not anyone related. Come on now, don't be thick, you're smarter than this."

My mind rolled. *He* asked Raven . . . oh hell . . . "You don't mean . . ."

"Please, you can say his name." He gave me a half bow, mocking me.

"Talan."

Raven grinned. "You see, I don't need to manipulate you, Talan's doing it enough for the both of us."

I was not truly surprised. I knew there were two people working against me, but for Peta's sake a small part of me had hoped Talan was not involved.

I took a deep breath. Shazer and Peta landed a few feet

behind me with a thud and a ruffling of feathers. The crowd gasped and pulled back, a low murmur rolling through them.

The last time they'd seen him was when I'd sunk the Eyrie, and it had been momentarily. We'd not stuck around long enough for anyone to really be star struck.

Samara sucked in a sharp breath. "Pegasus? I thought we were seeing things before. We thought you were an apparition in the aftermath of the destruction."

Shazer snorted and trotted past me. "My queen. I did not have time to chat last I was here."

I stiffened where I stood. He brushed past me as if I didn't exist. Peta whispered to him as they passed me.

"The necklace."

It felt as though the Sylphs had stolen my air as I watched him trot forward and bow at Samara's feet. She fluttered a hand to her chest as her eyes filled with tears. What in the name of the mother goddess was going on?

"If you are here, then our world is coming to an end," she whispered.

"I don't believe any of that horse shit," he said, flicking his head up once, but otherwise remaining on his bent knee. She approached him slowly, and it was only then I truly saw her.

The way she walked. The heavy slow steps, the swell of her belly, the way she cradled herself.

I whipped my head to the side and glared at Raven. He grinned and shrugged like a little boy caught with his hand in the cookie jar.

To fight with Samara was one thing; to battle her for the stone when she was pregnant—and obviously close to her time—was another entirely. He was banking on me being soft.

I hardened everything in me and slowly shook my head. His grin slipped, the silent communication only siblings had making my thoughts clear.

I would not back down. I would not hold back.

Samara shifted, drawing my eyes back to her. "Pegasus, the legends speak of you coming home." Her hands fluttered to her belly. "Of you being the messenger before the world is broken again. Is . . . that why you are here?"

Each word she spoke was weighted with a fear that was nearly visible in the thin mountain air.

"Nope." He lurched forward as he moved to stand, his muzzle grazing the flat of her chest. She didn't flinch, but closed her eyes as if she were in awe of him.

His velvet lips brushed her skin, and a sigh slipped out of her. He grabbed the necklace, the smoky diamond dangling from it, and reared back, snatching it from her neck.

The stone glittered as it sang through the air.

"Don't say I never gave you anything," Shazer crowed as he spun, spreading his wings and essentially b l o c k i n g Samara from seeing what he'd done.

I took two steps and held my hand out for the necklace.

Easier than any of the other retrievals, and no one got hurt.

And that's where I was so very, very wrong.

CHAPTER 19

aven whipped a hand out as the stone flickered through the air. "I think not."

The stone froze, above my head. I could have easily jumped and grabbed it. Could have fought him right there.

I lifted an eyebrow, though my heart pounded. I knew I couldn't beat him. We'd been down this path before. Raven was too strong; he had too much power in all five elements for me to face him again. But he didn't need to know how I felt.

"No? You need another boost of power to face me?"

He grinned, his eyes damn well sparkling. "Oh, I think you and I both know how that will end. You on the ground. Me sparing your life. Or not, maybe. I don't know exactly how that part would end." The necklace floated slowly to him. Shazer lunged for it and Raven flicked his fingers at the Pegasus.

His legs were sucked down into the stone as he leapt, the

momentum of his body bending him forward. The snap of bones as he fell rent the air. He didn't scream in pain, but grunted as he slumped. Peta snarled, leapt from his back and shifted. She crouched in front of Shazer, snarls rolling from her lips.

Raven snorted. "You want to play, kitty? Then let's play."

He grabbed the diamond from the air and snapped the fingers on his other hand. The stone disappeared, and Raven shifted. Literally shifted.

His body contorted, twisting in the blink of an eye into a monstrous grizzly bear. He was double the size of any regular grizzly, but worse, he was fast. Fast like a cat, with the power of a bear. He dropped to all fours and strode toward Shazer.

I knew without a shadow of a doubt he intended to tear Shazer apart. And he would go through Peta to do it. If I had to choose, I would, and it would always be her.

"Peta, back off!"

Samara cried out. "Lark, what is happening?"

"Not now, Samara, let me deal with one thing at a time." I pulled my spear from my side, already knowing how useless I was going to be. Peta darted around the side of Raven, slashing at him with her wicked claws. He roared, and was on her in a flash, a huge paw glancing off her hip. I called on the power of the earth to hold him down. To pin him.

Nothing happened. "Goblin shit." This was not the time to lose my connection to my elements, and I didn't have time to figure out why.

I ran at him, swinging my spear in a huge arc. I brought it down the back of his rump. The blade bounced off as if it were completely dull.

I called Spirit to weave around Earth.

Again, nothing happened. What the hell was

happening? I felt it then, in the space of a heartbeat. The same languorous sense I'd only received around one person. Talan.

He had to be blocking me.

"I'm blocking you both, to be fair." His voice spun me around. He stood against one of the pillars. "To keep things *even steven,* as the humans say."

"It's not even!"

"Yes, it is." He spoke as if he was urging me on. "Meet him on his terms, Lark."

I stumbled. On Raven's terms? I wasn't a shape shifter. I stared at Peta as she darted around Raven, landing blows, but unable to truly take him on her own.

Power of the heart, child. You have that. Use it. She is your soulmate for a reason. Littermate *might be a better term.*

The voice of the mountain rolled through me and I dropped my spear. Peta's image flooded my mind and I grasped hold of it, believing the words of the mountain. Believing I was more than I'd ever known.

The shift took me like lightning; between one step and the next I was no longer on two feet, but running on four. Flashes of gray and white on my legs were all I saw as I leapt toward the mountain of brown fur, a snarl ripping out of me. The rush of power coursing through me was like nothing I'd ever experienced, like nothing I'd ever known.

I landed on his back and gripped with all four feet, clinging to him like a monkey grips a branch. He roared and swept a paw back for me, but I was too high up for him to reach.

Peta dodged his intermittent blows as I dug in, biting through the thick hide as I sought his spine. A glorious battle rage rolled through me, a blood lust that blurred my thoughts until only a single image of his death burned inside my mind. I buried my fangs into him over and over as he bucked and writhed under me.

His body humped and we swung to the side. I dove to the other side, away from him as he rolled to his back in an attempt to squash me.

I leapt to stand beside Peta.

"Lark?"

I nodded, not sure I was able to speak like she could.

The smoky diamond was somewhere within his fur, I was sure of it. But where? I narrowed my eyes.

I ran at him while he fumbled on his back. Fast and powerful he might be as a bear, but he was also heavy on his back like a turtle flipped over. At the last second, I jumped, landing on his soft underbelly. I dug my claws in, pricking the skin like cutting through lard with a scorching-hot knife. He grunted under me and I tightened my hold. One good swipe and his innards would spill out.

Peta stalked beside us, speaking for me. "The stone. Your life for the stone."

Raven flexed as if he'd move and I slid my claws in further, tearing the flesh slowly. His eyes flicked to me, then back to Peta. He roared, but couldn't move without being mortally wounded, and he knew it.

Apparently it was true: I wasn't the only one blocked from using their elemental powers. At least Talan was fair in his own twisted way.

Raven's body trembled under me, and for the first time I saw fear in his eyes. Without his powers behind him, he was no safer than any other low-level elemental.

He shifted back to his elemental form, clothes intact, but I clung to him, my teeth bared. Still on his back, my claws were buried in his pale belly, blood bubbling up around the punctures from the three-inch-long daggers attached to me.

"The stone," Peta bit out. "Or she'll gut you right now."

A part of me wondered how far he'd push things, the other part wondered that Samara didn't help him. Then again, the Sylphs had stood by and let Cassava and me wreak havoc on their home without interference. He lifted one hand and slid it into his pants.

Just as slowly, he pulled his hand out and from it dangled the necklace. I leaned forward and grabbed it with my teeth. But I didn't take my claws from Raven.

His eyes widened. "You made a deal."

I tightened my claws on him, my thoughts raging. He'd been the cause of so much death, so much destruction. He was the reason I'd broken Keeda's mind, the reason I'd had to kill Vetch. He'd forced my hand to kill our father.

I glanced at Peta and nodded, the bond between us tighter than ever. She spoke for me. "You are hereby sentenced to death, Raven, as is Larkspur's right as an Ender and protector of the Rim."

I braced myself. He closed his eyes. "I know, Lark. I know."

Electricity blasted through me, sent me flying off Raven in a burst of light and pain.

I tumbled through the air and slammed into the ground next to where Shazer lay. Stunned, I lay unable to move as I processed what had happened.

"Samara, she stopped you," Shazer said. I glanced at him, saw the agony in his eyes. I could heal him.

"Get your shit done, fix my legs later." He grunted and closed his eyes. "Damn this body; you keep having to heal me and my fragile bits."

Raven stood, though he was far from steady and the blood ran freely from several wounds. He wobbled. "You surprise me, sister. I didn't think you had it in you."

I thought about standing on two feet and the shift slid through me as if I'd been doing it all my life. A feeling of desperation rolled through me as I reached once more for my connection to Spirit and Earth. They sang through me, hot and wild. A sigh of relief slipped from me.

Raven smiled at me, but it was weak. "Before this goes any further, I think you should meet someone."

He took a few limping steps toward Samara. She backed up, holding a hand out to him. "Stay where you are. I saved you only for the sake of our child." Wind powered between them, blowing his hair back and out of its perfect slicked coif.

"Samara, please." Lines of power coursed up his arms, a vibrant pink that gave him away. "You love me."

Her eyes softened and she relaxed once more. "I do love you. You're the father of my baby."

My gag reflex lurched at the sickeningly sweet words.

"Raven, your mommy dearest, Cassava to be clear, can't be too happy you've left her for someone younger." I took a step, beckoning Peta to come to me. I didn't want her any closer to him than she had to be.

Raven shrugged, but his eyes were far from worried. In fact, they looked downright happy with the way they sparkled. Happy.

This did not bode well.

"You have the stone, but I have something to show you. Something I have on loan from my mother." He held one fist up over his head and let out a long, high-pitched whistle. There were no lines of power on his arms, no indication that he did anything but whistle. And yet, something in his stance, the look in his eyes told me I wasn't going to like what he had to show me.

The whoosh of wings drew my eyes upward. A bird

rushed downward, a huge big bird. What the hell was Raven's game now?

The bird, an eagle I could easily see now that it was close, landing on Raven's arm.

"Do you like him? I must say Mother was rather clever when she captured him."

I glanced at Peta, who shrugged.

Shazer gave a low groan. "Lark, don't give him the stone."

"I'm not." I clutched the smoky diamond tighter as if it would otherwise slip from my fingers.

Raven grinned, the blood on his face and belly still dripping, but he acted like it meant nothing. "No, I think you'll give me the stone. I think you'll give me all the stones you have."

None of this made sense. None of it.

I took a step. "You are sentenced to death, Raven. This ends."

"You aren't strong enough to kill me. You had your chance." His free hand touched his belly gingerly. "And you let it slip by."

He patted the eagle on top of his head, rather roughly. More like hitting than patting. "A nice, golden eagle. Lovely. Much better than he was before, wouldn't you agree?"

Golden eagle.

When it is done, I will help you find your golden eagle.

The mother goddess's words went off like a bomb inside my head. Not possible, this was not possible.

"No."

"You can say no all you want." Raven continued to smack the eagle I refused to think of as Ash. "But the truth is the truth."

The eagle turned honey gold eyes to me. I would know those eyes and the feel of them on mine if I were blind.

"No." It was the only thing I could say, the only word I had left to me. Ash had to be a shifter, then, that was the only other answer. Even though I knew I was wrong the second I thought it.

"To answer a coming question, no, he's not a shifter. Mother confined him to this form, though why she didn't just kill him I can't fathom. Then again, it will work in my favor now, I think." He flexed his arm and sent Ash back into the sky. The eagle circled once, let out a piercing cry that struck through me, and winged away.

"He was delivering a message for me. He's Mother's messenger boy now. But I would give him to you, for the stones." Raven grinned.

Time paused, the world slowed, my heart stopped beating, I couldn't move. Couldn't breathe or think. I had two powers to me, two elements that were mine. And one of them would allow me to control Raven.

I grabbed hold of Spirit and held it like never before.

I was ending this. Now.

CHAPTER 20

Raven's eyes widened. "What are you doing?"

I slammed Spirit into him, using it like the weapon it was, digging it into his mind. He stumbled back and shook his head, tried to lift a hand, red lines of power coursing over his skin. Fire at his fingertips.

"No." I threw the word at him and he lowered his hand, horror finally replacing the smug look on his lips.

Spirit grew in me, filling me as fast as I flung it at Raven. I wanted control over him, I wanted him to break into a thousand pieces at my feet and beg for his life. Beg to be forgiven so I could tell him it would never happen. Then and only then would I kill him.

"Larkspur, this is not the way." Talan stepped between Raven and me. I felt Talan's hold on Spirit, felt him trying to slow me down. I flicked a hand at him, and the ground bucked under his feet, sending him to his knees. I thought it would break his concentration. I was wrong.

"You're on his side?" Peta cried out, her pain cutting

through me. Chaos built around us, so many emotions, so much power, so much pain.

Raven shook his head and I screamed, a wordless cry as I threw everything I had at him. "Tell the truth, Raven. Do it."

His mouth flopped open, once, twice and then the words came in a flood.

"I don't love Samara. I manipulated her with Spirit to accept me into her bed. I plan to let her carry to term, have the baby, and then I will use her own Enders to kill her. They will think she is dangerous to her family and they will kill her. I will raise the child on my own and take control of the throne. Once that is done I will take the Rim next. I will keep Bella as my queen. She reminds me of Mother. We will take each family throne, one at a time. But I will do it this time, I will not rule through others. I will rule. I will bring the elementals into line."

The Sylphs around us gasped and shifted. "Samara, do you hear this?"

"I hear it." She stepped beside me and laid a hand on my arm. "You will kill him?"

"Yes."

Raven shook and I refocused on him. Talan stood where I'd thrown him.

"Lark, this is not the way. Do you not feel it, the darkening of your soul?"

I didn't care that he was right, that I did feel my heart closing off. The part of me that would have held back and given mercy slowly shriveled.

I snorted. "It is not the use of Spirit that darkens me, but this world and those who are in it. Raven, is that all the truth?"

He shuddered, his body twitching. "You were always my

favorite, Lark. I wanted us to be on the same side through this all. I didn't want to hurt you."

His words surprised and hurt me more than I thought they would have. I stared at him, his blue eyes fighting sudden tears. I hardened every part of me. "Then you should have tried harder to do what was right."

He bowed his head and slumped to the ground. The second his knees hit the stone he disappeared.

A scream of fury ripped from my mouth.

I stumbled forward. I knew he'd had that trick up his sleeve, but I'd thought he'd be too busy fending me off to use it. Damn it all to the seventh hell.

A hand touched my arm and I swung around to face the deep blue eyes of Talan. "He held back, do you realize that? He didn't use all his power, though maybe he didn't even realize it. I think a part of him wanted to tell you the truth all along. Whatever bond you have with him from the past still affects him now. It could play into your favor at some point."

I jerked away from him with a snarl. "You stay the hell away from me." I dug my hand into the leather pouch at my side and produced the plastic bracelet he'd offered me. I flung it at his feet.

Peta let out a long, low hiss and shook her head. "You've turned out poorly, Talan. You obviously needed me more than you realized."

As I spun away, I caught the look of sorrow in his eyes. "Peta, you don't understand."

I left them to argue. I had a queen to face. Samara had sunk to the ground, her skirts pooling around her.

"Lark, what did he do to me?"

I crouched in front of her. "Manipulation. He has a powerful tool that he used to benefit himself."

Her pale eyes widened and her mouth dropped open. "He could do it again?"

I nodded. "He could. You need all your people to know to send a message for me immediately if he returns. If they are all aware, he won't be able to control all of them at once."

She grabbed my hands. "He'll come for my baby."

I gripped her tightly. "No, I don't think so." At least not right away, but I wasn't going to worry her with that now.

Samara slumped farther, then slowly straightened herself. "The stone?"

I lied, knowing it would be easier for her to give it up. "I believe it was how he manipulated you. I didn't know it was possible." I didn't want to tell her that she'd been manipulated not only by Raven using Spirit, but by some other unknown elemental that had his own agenda via the smoky diamond. No need to have her panic that there was more than one manipulator of epic proportions out there.

With a quick nod, she held her hands out to me, and I helped her stand.

"Larkspur has once more saved our family. If ever she needs help, you are to give it. If ever she is in danger, you will try to save her. She is a protector not only of the Rim, but of the Eyrie as well. Raven will be killed on sight."

The crowd murmured and agreed, though I saw more than one pair of eyes narrow on me.

I moved away from her, hurrying to Shazer. I laid my hands on him, not caring how much of my soul darkened to heal him. Spirit flowed through me and into him, weaving the bones back together. Shazer let out a low groan. "Damn, that hurts almost as much as breaking them."

"I could leave them as is," I said through gritted teeth.

He lurched up to his feet. "Thanks, but I rather like being able to stand."

The Sylphs who'd been so reluctant closed ranks around him, petting his side and touching his feathers. He gave me a wink. "I think they like me."

"Vanity will get you nowhere," Peta said. "You're still a horse's ass."

He let out a whinny and the Sylphs around him giggled and sighed.

I took a few steps back, allowing Shazer whatever hero worship he had coming.

Samara stepped beside me once more. "He is legend here. The soul of air made flesh."

"He's a good friend," I said. But my mind was already away from Shazer and whatever legend he represented.

Unfortunately, I knew Talan was right. For some reason, Raven left rather than battle me. Whether it was out of some sort of kindness or a way to drag things out between us, I didn't know.

At least Raven had spilled his proverbial guts, and now I knew what his plans had been, not that it was likely to help me any. The thing I couldn't figure out was that while he'd asked for the stones, it had been . . . offhand. And he'd not tried to really fight me for them.

I looked around for Talan, but he was gone.

They were a couple of cowards as far as I was concerned. I walked away from the crowd, Peta with me. A thought I didn't like rolled around in my head, making me question not only what I'd learned, but the premise I was running on.

"Did you notice Raven didn't talk much about the stones? He asked, but he hadn't even taken the smoky diamond from Samara," I said.

Peta glanced up at me. "What does that matter?"

I frowned. "The mother goddess said Raven wanted

the stones for himself, that I was hunting them at the same time as him. But he was never really hunting for them. He was just hanging out in the Eyrie, sending Enders after me, waiting for me to come to him. Causing trouble, yes, but . . . it just doesn't add up. If he'd wanted the stones, why didn't he fight harder?" I rubbed a hand over my face, a new line of thought making me break out in a sudden cold sweat.

What if I was wrong about Talan? What if I was wrong about Raven?

What if there was a third player I'd not truly ever considered? A person I trusted, a person who'd guided and at the same time manipulated me all along?

Horror clutched at my belly as the pieces fell into place in a wicked, dangerous way. An impossibility that I'd never considered before rose and looked me straight in the eye with the malevolence of a red-eyed demon.

"We have to go, right now," I whispered to Peta.

"What? Why?"

I opened my mouth to tell her, but the horror of the words was too much. Too much and too painful to truly believe.

But the more they rolled around in my head, the more I knew they were the truth.

The truth hurt, and this burned like a thousand hot pokers being jammed into my belly. I'd been a fool, a stupid trusting fool, and the hurt slowly formed into an anger that burned away the pain.

"Lark?" Peta clawed at my leg in an attempt to slow me.

"Now, we have to go now," I said again.

She let go of me. "If you are sure."

"I am." I strode across the Eyrie toward the Pegasus. "Shazer, are you ready to fly?"

"Yeah," Peta snipped. "You done with your fan club?"

Surprisingly, the Sylphs laughed as he backed away from them. "Don't blame me for being beautiful."

I leapt onto his back, Peta right behind me. Samara hurried to my side and put a hand on my leg. "Lark, will you come when the baby is born?"

I didn't want to make promises I couldn't keep. What I was about to do was beyond dangerous; it was downright suicidal, and I knew it, no matter how much my anger fueled me.

"I will try."

"I want you to be his guardian. To be his protector as you've been mine." Her eyes welled and I placed a hand on hers. It occurred to me then that the next generation was going to be full of half-breed royals. More than ever before. They needed the elemental world to be ready for them and their strength.

"I will try," I repeated. "I . . . may not be here."

Her eyes closed. "Be safe then, for I believe you may hold the world in your hands."

A chill swept through me. "Advice, or insight?"

Her eyes fluttered open. "Aria left me the gift of sight. It comes now and again. Our world needs you alive, Lark. For whatever is coming is worse than even the demon hordes." She shuddered and took her hand from mine. I gritted my teeth on the chill that made them want to chatter.

Shazer took a leap, and the Sylphs around us swept us upward on a monster gust of wind. He laughed and his wings beat to keep the momentum going. "I think I like them."

Another time I would have laughed. But not now. Not with what I knew I was going to do.

"Where are we going exactly?" he asked. Peta looked up at me, concern filling her eyes. I knew she could feel the anxiety growing in me, the fear and the feeling of inevitability. The knowledge that I was most likely walking into a trap, and a bad one at that.

I closed my eyes and let my mind relax, thinking about where I needed to go. I had all the stones, all of them. That was a lie, but it didn't matter. I knew she would believe me. I'd never tried to lie to her before. A picture floated across my mind, the hanging trees, the thick moss, the stagnant water and rotting trees. Why was I not surprised at what I was seeing? Finley said Cassava took Ash to the same place. The irony was not lost on me.

"The cypress swamps."

Shazer didn't argue, just swept us back to the North American continent. I pulled Peta into my arms and buried my face in her thick fur. Her front legs swept around my neck in a hug, her paws kneading the back of my head. "Lark, I have never felt fear like this in you."

I lifted my head. "Shazer."

"Yeah?" He was oblivious to my distress. That was about to change.

"When we land, I want you to fly back to the Eyrie."

"What? Why?"

I locked eyes with Peta and she slowly nodded. "I am with you, Lark. Never doubt it."

Shazer shook his head. "Talk, woman, or I'll dump you off my back right here."

"I think I know who is behind everything. I know who made the stones, I know who made you. And she's still playing us." I whispered the words, as if she could hear us. For all I knew, she could.

He seemed to stall mid-air, his wings stilling as he stared back at me, understanding slowly dawning. "No. You can't possibly mean her."

I nodded slowly. "Yes. I think . . . I think the mother goddess is not who she seems to be."

And I was about to face her not as a child of hers, not as a favored chosen one.

But as an opponent and a rival to her power.

CHAPTER 21

Shazer flew hard and fast, never stopping once. As if we had a demon tailing us with our names engraved on his sword. Yet it wasn't what was behind us that hurried his wings.

My request for speed was the only reason he flew as fast and as hard as he did.

"Why would you hurry?" he called out between gulps of air.

"Because she thinks I believe we are on a deadline, and that Raven is behind us, chasing us. I doubt that is the case now, but I need whatever surprise I can get. I will pretend I know nothing." I had a hand on the leather pouch at my side. Four of the five stones rested there. The fifth was still buried under Griffin's hut—the pink diamond that controlled Spirit.

The cypress swamps swept into view on the horizon as the sun rose behind us, dispelling the long night. My legs ached from gripping Shazer's sides and the anxiety that filled me was almost too much to contain. For a split second, I wished I could have someone at my side. Not Ash, though, and that surprised me.

Raven. He was strong enough that maybe with the two of us working together we could stop her.

What the hell was I thinking? Exhaustion was making me stupid, that was the only answer. Shazer brought us to a bare section of beach, landing and dropping immediately to his knees. He blew out a long breath.

"I cannot fly back to the Eyrie. I must rest." He groaned and flopped onto his side, his wings stretching out behind him.

"Go as soon as you can. At least . . . get away from here."

He raised his head. "Ash will be trapped forever as an eagle if you die here."

I took a deep breath. "Then I leave that in your charge. Tell Samara, maybe she can help . . . if I don't make it."

Peta stood in the sand beside me, shifting into her leopard form. "We must hurry."

Her unspoken words were as clear. If we wanted the ruse to hold, we had to move as though we believed we were being chased by Raven. I had one more thing to do, though. I went to my knees beside Shazer and opened the leather pouch. From it I poured all the stones, sorting them into two piles.

"What are you doing?" Shazer asked.

"If I die, you hold the key to defeating her," I whispered. "I do not know who you will trust, but I trust you."

I hurried, my hands shook, and I knew this was the only chance I had to beat her. A gamble was ahead of me, and I was banking everything on it.

A curse.

The stones.

The mother goddess. I prayed I was right.

I nodded and we jogged across the small patch of sand and into the cover of the trees. The dense vegetation pulled at me. I let it for a bit before connecting with Earth to move things enough that the path was clear. Peta frowned up at me. I couldn't explain now, we were too close.

But if I was truly in a hurry, I wouldn't think about my connection to the earth, not right away. At least, that was the game I was playing. We sloshed through the water. "Peta—"

"I know, Lark. I know." She pressed herself against my leg. We could both die, we both knew it. At least . . . at least she was with me.

The anxiety eased when the truth of it settled on my heart. I would never be alone, Peta would never cast me away as so many people had done in my life. Not even for Talan.

A soft rumbling purr rolled through her and into me. I dropped my hand to her head and let the last of the anxiety flow out of me, and in its place my confidence grew.

I had a plan, it was a good one. Maybe we could pull this off.

My next step sunk me in brown swamp water up to my chest. I sucked in a sharp breath as something slithered between my legs. Peta swam ahead of me, her ears pinned back. "Keep an eye out for logs with eyes."

She grunted and kept swimming. The pull to the center of the swamp didn't let up, and I followed it.

The water stunk, the rank, acrid scent of death that had resided for too long above ground filled my lungs. I hurried to get out of the water as much as to reach my destination.

"Almost there." Peta tipped her head at what was in front of us.

A curtain of moss curled down from the trees in various shades of pale green. Situated out of the water, the land looked solid, though I had no doubt there was more water than soil under it.

I approached the moss divider, each step bringing me farther out of the water until I stood on—somewhat—dry land. I glanced at Peta, she nodded, and I stepped forward, my hand lifted to the moss. It parted on its own, without any direction from me. Beyond the moss was a crystal clear pool of water. Even at that distance I could see it was pristine, unlike the rest of the swamp. The mother goddess sat beside it, her back to me.

Once more she had taken the image of my mother. I swallowed hard.

"Lark, you have the stones? Did you use the fake ones to replace the real ones?" she asked softly, though she already had the answer.

"Yes." I didn't dare take another step. She raised her head and smiled at me, my mother's smile, my mother's face. "You put the fake stones in the grave then? The grave that was Ash's."

She tipped her head to one side. "I knew you would not just believe he was gone, that you would find a way to prove to yourself he was alive if I sent you in that direction. I had your father place the stones with the body when it was buried. You are, if nothing else, predictable."

I gave a slow nod, doing my best to school my face. "Did we make it in time?"

"Yes, barely, but yes. Raven is close behind you." Her

eyes crinkled with pleasure. My heart and gut lurched. "Bring them to me, let me see them."

With leaden feet I did as she asked, walking until I was only a few feet in front of her. I undid the leather pouch from my belt and handed it to her. "What happens now?"

She opened the pouch and peered in, the smile widening on her face. "Oh, little Larkspur. Your desire to fit in, to be the good girl. It will be the death of you, I think."

I took several steps back, hating that I'd been right. A minuscule piece of me had still believed I could be wrong. That my mistrust was misplaced. It died with nary a whimper.

Peta stayed at my side as I moved back, sticking to me like a burr.

The mother goddess glanced up at me. "Do you know the stones can be manipulated by those who control Spirit?"

What was she trying to say? "The one who created them, you mean."

"Not just the creator." She clutched the bag close to her. "No, they can be used by anyone who is strong in Spirit."

"Like Raven." I spat his name out.

"No, he is not strong enough with Spirit. I think you could do it if you put your mind to it, and had the training. Talan, of course, is the one I speak of. He can use the stones to control things."

Her words were yet another nail in Talan's coffin. "He warned the rulers I was coming?"

She nodded. "And told them to fight like demons."

"Why would he do that?" I truly didn't understand him or his intentions.

She jiggled the leather bag, the sound of the stones clinking softly in the air. I held my breath, but she didn't seem to notice anything. "He believes the stones are dangerous and should not be held by anyone. I, on the other hand, believe they are the tools they were created to be."

I shrugged, trying to act like I didn't feel the undertone to her words. "I'm not terribly surprised he did that. He's an asshole."

Her eyebrows raised in tandem. "You don't like him?"

I shook my head. "No. I don't."

"Pity, he could have helped you, if you'd let him." She smiled again, but the smile darkened until it was no longer my mother's smile. I gritted my teeth.

"I want to tell you a story, Larkspur. It will help things make sense to you. Many years ago these stones were created by an elemental who was more than she seemed to be." Her eyes glossed over a little. "She was punished by those who sought to take away her power. As you know, being the strongest of our people is a dangerous position to be in."

I nodded, and struggled to swallow past the growing tightness in my throat.

She held the leather pouch. "She was punished for being strong, Lark. Cursed for it. The stones were taken from her, and a Spirit Walker convinced a witch to weave a spell. Only when all five stones were brought back to the elemental would the curse be broken. She tried once to bring the stones back to her, but the draw to them was too strong for those elementals she asked for help. Cassava. Raven. They both kept the stones when they were to give them to her."

I frowned, though her story lined up with what I knew. Of course, I was the tool she'd been waiting for. The elemental who would be obedient even when it took power from me. "And the curse? What was it?"

"That she could not attack another elemental. She

252

couldn't use her power to directly influence anything." She smiled at me, and gave a slow wink. "That will change now. I needed you and Raven both in the beginning, Lark. I played you both, using you to do my work for me. But now that I have the stones, I can take my rightful place. I do not need you anymore."

I took a step back and reached for my two elements. They slid through my fingers like water through sand. A block, she'd put a block on me. I took another step back.

The mother goddess smiled at me. "If you'd been more obedient, I'd let you live. But you are a typical child of Spirit. Always looking for trouble. Helping the supernaturals, stopping the demons with them. I'm sorry, Lark, but you are going to die now. Raven, of course, will take the blame. Or perhaps Talan, since you so dislike him."

She said it all so matter-of-factly. Like we were discussing the weather.

"Why would you give Peta to me, then? Why would you help me?" I took another step back.

She waved a hand at me and jiggled the leather bag with the other. "I needed you to survive long enough to do what I needed you to do. Peta is the only familiar that has the training to keep you alive." She paused and tipped her head. "You were my backup plan in case Raven fell through."

"You mean so I could find the stones."

Viv, I suppose she was never the mother goddess after all, nodded. "And you threw the families into disarray which was an added bonus. The chaos you provide will be a perfect catalyst for me to step in. I am known as the mother goddess. Which family will turn from me?"

"So all that crap about me being a chosen one?"

"You had no confidence, and I needed strength from

you. I needed you to believe in yourself. Only you took it a tad bit too far; you grew far stronger than I thought you would."

The crack of a branch whipped me around. I had my spear up and poised for an attack before I registered who it was.

Talan stepped into the clearing, and though he approached me his eyes were trained on Viv. "You don't want to tell her the rest?"

She glared at him. "You have been a thorn in my side for too long, Talan. Perhaps you should die with her. Suiting, since you so cared for Ulani, that you should die at her daughter's side."

He grinned at her. "I think you're about to gain a new thorn." He glanced at me. "Smart move."

I kept my face carefully blank, as if I didn't have a clue what he was talking about. Idiot, he was going to blow my ruse. If he'd noticed what I'd done, the only question was, would she?

Viv lifted a hand. "She is going to die, Talan. And you will be next if you care to stand there and vex me."

He laughed softly. "Oh, I don't think it's going to be as easy as you think. You broke the bond between Peta and me on purpose. Why?"

Peta gasped. "No, that can't be."

I stood there with my mouth hanging open. "She could do that?"

"Yes, she can. If I'd been able to find Peta, I would have gone after her. Viv broke my ability to do that, though, and for many years, I thought Peta was dead. As she thought I was." He didn't take his eyes off Viv. "You see, she believed that without my loyal cat, I would be open to danger and easier to kill. Spirit walkers are nothing if not prone to an early death. All the charges Peta was sent to . . . they were marked for death. So that she would believe she was a poor familiar. You changed all that for her, Lark."

Viv glared at him, and the glamor I'd always associated with her slowly drifted away, the last of my belief system collapsing around me. Her long dark brown hair and deep brown eyes were those of a Terraling. She looked disturbingly like Cassava.

That wasn't what bothered me, though.

The truth fell on me, crushing a piece of my heart and spirit. We were alone then in this world; there was no mother goddess to turn to, no gentle love to guide us. No, that was not true. There was something out there. I just wasn't sure exactly what the voice of the mountain was.

Talan stood to the left of me, his hands tucked behind his back. "Lark, what she doesn't want you to know is she is not a mix of elements like Raven. She is a true hybrid, like you. She is—"

"Shut your mouth!" She flung a hand at him, I saw the lines of power over her arms. White and blue twinned across her skin. The intent was clear as day. She was going to kill him.

I may not have liked him, but I couldn't let him die. Not if he wasn't what I thought. I leapt at him, tackling him to the ground as the power ripped over our heads. Talan rolled and we were both on our knees in a flash.

"Come on, Viv. Let's see what you've got." He taunted her, beckoning with his one hand with a wiggle of his fingers.

"Are you crazy?"

"No, I trust you."

His words shocked me. He trusted me? I didn't trust him any further than I would trust Raven. Well, maybe a bit more than I trusted Raven.

Viv raised her hand a second time and Talan held a hand out to me. "Stay back. In case I'm wrong."

She snarled. "You are done. But I'm killing her first. To be sure that she does not interfere, yet again." The power built in the air, the small hairs on my arms stood at attention. Time slowed. Peta leapt into my arms, her body covering mine.

"Where you go, I go. I trust you." Her eyes never left mine and I stared into her face.

Even into death. I wrapped my arms around her, hoping I'd done the right thing. Praying to a deity I no longer believed existed. I lifted my eyes.

Viv flung both hands at us and the world seemed to pause further. The lines of power intensified on her, flaring, and then a boom of thunder filled the tiny space. It felt as though all five elements screamed at once, the sound of death and destruction, inferno and hurricane, earthquake and rogue waves swept into a single note that made my heart waver. I clung to Peta, tucking my head against her, sure it was our death I felt.

But the sound faded and I slowly opened my eyes. Peta trembled, and her big green eyes blinked up at me. "Are we still alive?"

Talan stood off to one side, his eyes at half-mast, and his hands on his hips.

"What the hell happened?" I slid Peta off my lap and stood.

"The curse," he said. "You didn't give her the real stones, so when she attacked you, the curse kicked into overdrive. How . . . how did you know she was the one who'd created the stones? It took me years to figure out she wasn't the mother goddess."

I blinked, unable to clear my vision completely. Where

Viv had been was nothing but a charred piece of ground. "Is she dead?"

He walked to the burn mark and scuffed a foot over it. "I doubt it. Hurt probably, and pissed as Peta was when I threw her into that arctic lake, but not dead. How did you know?"

Peta sniffed. "I was not pissed. I was cold, you fool."

I stood under the cypress trees, the rot of the swamp curling around me. I drew it into my lungs. "How did she not know the stones were fake? I mean, I'm glad she didn't, but is she really that full of herself?"

Talan shrugged. "Pride is a funny thing. And she trusted you to be obedient. So why would she even bother checking?"

That was along the lines I'd been thinking, hoping would happen. "She told me Raven was searching for the stones, but he wasn't. He was having a good time in the Eyrie. I knew you were also causing problems, but it . . . I don't know. I just knew. In the Eyrie, I knew. The story about the old elemental, about the stones, about Shazer." I said the Pegasus's name and I froze. "Worm shit, what if something happened to Shazer when I hurt her?" I bolted through the swamp as quickly as I could. Peta leapt along beside me. "Go, Peta, you're faster."

She didn't wait, but sped through the swamp ahead of me.

Talan ran at my side, slipping and sliding, but he didn't argue with me. And for the first time since I'd met him, he didn't just disappear on me. "Why would she have hurt him?"

"Because she made him. She created him." I pushed through the last of the foliage and burst onto the sandy beach. The sun beat down, brilliant and hot. Shazer was flopped out on his side, unmoving, the feathers of his wings ruffling in a breeze off the water the only movement.

Peta was at his head. She smacked him with a paw three times in the space of a second. "Wake up."

He jerked and blinked several times, his large dark eyes foggy with sleep. Cracking a big yawn, he looked around. "Tell me we aren't off to somewhere else."

I slumped where I stood. "She didn't hurt you?"

"Why would she hurt me?" He sat up and the lower part of his mane rolled forward. The material from Bella's skirt rolled forward as it came undone. Four stones glittered as they fell to the sand. I scooped them up and wrapped them once more into the green cloth. I tied the knot tighter, pulling it hard before I tucked the package under my vest.

Talan leaned forward, his hands on his thighs as a laugh boomed out of him. "Well, I'll be damned."

I glared at him. "To be clear, we are not friends. You manipulated the leaders to attack me, didn't you?"

He stood and his lips tightened a moment. "You need to be humble to be teachable, Lark. You are anything but. And I *need* you to learn. The world will depend on your ability to learn and to grow with what you have been given."

I snorted. "I've heard that line before. Viv used it on me more than once. So you'd best come up with something better than that to convince me you are anything but an asshole on a power trip."

Shazer yawned again. I waved at him. "Go back to sleep."

He wasted no time in flopping back to the sand, wriggling his body to get in deeper.

I walked down the beach a ways, and Peta hurried to my side. "What now?"

What now indeed? "I think I have a rather powerful

enemy. Worse than Cassava ever was. Worse than Raven." I rubbed a hand over my face.

"You could be stronger than her," Talan said. I turned on my heel to face him.

"I doubt that. She has all five elements at her disposal. I can't use the stones; she could manipulate me. Shit, you could manipulate me."

He nodded. "You have the same ability she does. Did you not hear me? She was a Terraling Spirit walker hybrid. That is a particular brand of elemental."

"Why?"

His dark blue eyes never left mine. "You said it yourself: she is a powerful enemy. One that as soon as her wounds are healed will be hunting you down. She might not be able to hurt you directly, but will Raven fall to her lies again now that you ousted him from the Eyrie? Do you think Cassava could be twisted again if she was given the pink diamond? Or maybe Viv will find someone new to do her dirty business. Tell them that they are the chosen one. That she believes in them."

His words struck a chord with me I didn't like.

Fear crawled up and down my spine, biting and nipping. And then came the anger. "And, let me guess, your training will help me survive?"

"Yes."

Peta stepped between us, and her anger felt like my own. "Talan."

His eyes dipped to her. He smiled and crouched. "Will you forgive me?"

She tipped her head. "No. You've been an ass to Lark."

His head lowered. "Nepeta, you don't understand—"

"No, I don't. You weren't an ass when I left you." The

word was firm from her. "I wanted to believe Lark was wrong. That you weren't causing problems—"

"It has to be done," he said. "She has to be humble in order for Spirit to truly bind to her. You know that."

"Not like this. You're a fool. You always were when it came to understanding women and what made them tick."

I had to bite my lower lip to keep from laughing. His eyes shot to mine and he gave me the barest of headshakes. Almost like he was trying not to laugh too. Maybe it was the situation, I wasn't sure, but I liked him a little better for that. For being a fool and letting Peta chastise him.

She sat at my feet, her rounded ears flipped partway back. She lifted a paw and pushed it into his chest, shoving him onto his butt. "You need lessons yourself. You apologize for being an ass, right now."

Like she was his mother. I bit the inside of my cheeks and focused on breathing slowly, keeping the laughter under control.

"Nepeta, please. This is ridiculous."

Her ears went flat to her head and she bared her teeth at him. "Apologize."

He stood and took a step so she couldn't see his face. And he grinned at me wide enough that I could see the sincerity in it. The fool.

"Peta is right. I've been an ass." His grin never slipped. "Will you come with me? Will you let me help you?"

"You did not apologize. You only said you'd been an ass, which is true, but not an apology." She swatted at him with a big paw and he leapt back.

"Peta, I wasn't finished."

My chest shook with silent laughter. Peta's tail twitched. "Apologize or I will assume you truly meant her harm and then I will forget you were ever my charge and assume you are an enemy to us both."

She was serious. And I felt it then through our bond. She was going to attack him if he didn't apologize. The laughter evaporated from me, and along with it the last of the fear that she would choose Talan over me.

She stood, and the fur along her back rose as a low rumble rolled out of her. The mirth on his face slid off.

His jaw ticked and he held up both hands. "Larkspur, will you accept my apology?"

"Fine." I turned my back on him. Peta grabbed my leg and I yelped. "What?"

"When someone apologizes, you accept it properly."

Etiquette lessons from Peta was not something I was expecting. I sighed. "You're forgiven. And no, I don't want to train with you. I'm going home."

I started down the beach once more.

Of course, that wasn't the end of things with Talan.

He called after me.

"Ulani wanted you to train with me, and I promised her I would. I promised her I would watch over you and do all I could to help you learn. To keep you alive."

Ulani . . . my mother. I closed my eyes and pressed the heels of my hands to them. Damn it, what did I do now?

 e landed in the Rim late the next day. Talan rode behind me on Shazer's back, Peta between us. She purred so much, she drooled in her sleep.

"I was not drooling." She glared at me, even while she licked her lips.

I glanced at Talan, who shrugged. "Good luck convincing her."

It was nice she was so happy. I, on the other hand, was not as impressed with the outcome of things.

Talan would say nothing more about my mother after he'd dropped her name. "I'll tell you when you agree to train with me."

Asshole.

And he'd insisted on coming with me.

"Viv could come at you at any time. You need whatever help you can get now." He slid from Shazer's back first. "So stop moping."

My back stiffened. "I was not moping. I'm angry. There is a difference. Or are you struggling with your ability to read women again?"

Peta choked and laughed. "Oh, this is going to be fun."

"That is not the word I'd use," I muttered.

I had one goal in mind: get the pink diamond from Griffin's hut so I would know all five stones were safe from being used against me.

I strode in the direction of his home on the outer edge of the Rim near the ravine. I'd taken only three steps when Griffin appeared, coming from the Spiral. Bella and Flint were to one side of him. Griffin saw me and his normally smiling lips tightened.

Shit, I'd knocked his consort on her ass. "Griffin, it was not my fault. I didn't know—"

"You should have told me you stuffed the pink stone in my hut, yeah?" He lifted an eyebrow at me.

"I thought it was better the fewer people who knew. Wait . . . how did you know?"

"Viv had someone steal it from me."

My guts clenched and I closed my eyes. "Damn."

Bella looked from me to Griffin. "Who is Viv?"

"Long story." I ran a hand over my head and grabbed the back of my neck. I didn't know what to do, where to start. That was a first for me. Always the path ahead of me was laid out, a journey I knew I needed to take.

I glanced at Peta and she shook her head slowly. "I don't know."

Talan cleared his throat. "I do. This is the lull before the storm, Lark. Tell me you don't feel the world tensing?"

I stared at him, weighing his words and letting his meaning truly reach me. Under them was a truth I'd been ignoring. Part of the reason the mother goddess had convinced me she spoke truly of the world being destroyed was because I'd felt the same truth already. A humming fear deep within the earth that resonated through me. The world was in trouble, and I knew it in every molecule of my flesh and bone.

Child.

I flinched and looked around. Everyone's eyes widened at once. "I'm not the only one hearing this?"

A slow shake of heads sucked the air from my lungs. "Yes?"

Listen to him. He speaks the truth, and you will need his training. The Sylph named you right, Destroyer. But in destruction is new life. Remember that, if you remember nothing else.

The words faded, but the truth remained. I was not done with Talan, no matter how I wished he would just bugger off and pester someone else.

"The training?" I made myself ask.

"You will come with me. Leave everything behind."

Peta bristled and Shazer stomped a foot. I lifted an eyebrow. "They will follow."

"Your familiars can come, of course." He smiled. "But no one else."

Bella sucked in a breath, but she remained silent.

Going with Talan, training with him would mean leaving not only my family behind, but Ash too. He was still trapped as a golden eagle, waiting on someone to free him. I was the only one who even knew Cassava had him as a pet. My heart felt as though it were being torn in two. Training . . . as an Ender I understood the importance. The need to be truly prepared for battle.

I had to believe Ash would understand too. That he would be safe a little while longer.

But he wasn't the only one waiting on me. I closed my

eyes. Bramley might be out there too. Alive. Dead. Which one, I wouldn't know until I searched for him, until I found him and brought him home.

"You can help all those you love more if you have the strength and training to protect them," Talan said, his voice soft.

I clenched my hands into fists, fighting the urge to fight him. To deny him even though a part of me knew he was right. To tell him I could do it my way and survive. That was how I'd always done things. I'd fought the way I'd believed was right. It had worked up until now.

But . . . this time I wasn't so sure.

"I will . . . go with you." The words came out far softer than I'd wanted.

Talan nodded. "Then we leave now."

Shazer groaned. "Seriously?"

I touched Bella's hand. "I'll be back."

"I know," she whispered, tears tracking down her cheeks. She caught me around the neck and kissed each of my cheeks. "Do what you must, Lark. I trust you."

I turned to Flint. "Lark." Just my name, and I turned to Talan.

This was for them, to protect those I loved. To save them from Viv and what plans she had.

I mounted Shazer, Peta right behind me. Talan leapt astride, his arms locking around me. Shazer bolted down the length of the Rim and launched into the air with a powerful leap.

We circled and Talan's arms tightened further around me in a vise-like grip.

"You can do nothing. You have to train to help her," he said, his voice firm.

What was he talking about? Peta let out a pain-filled meow and I looked to where she stared.

Bella gazed up at me, her eyes filled with tears, her hand lifted in a wave.

And behind her wavered the image of the mother goddess. Viv. I lurched forward as if to throw myself from Shazer's back. Talan's arms tightened around my middle, clamping my arms to my sides.

"Forgive me, Lark. This is for the best." Spirit coiled around me, dampening my mind. I slumped into him, exhaustion overcoming me as my eyes slipped shut. "I hate you."

"I know," he whispered from far away. "I know. But you won't one day. One day you'll thank me."

Nothing more and the darkness took me, and in it I heard Viv laughing, heard her words as clearly as if she stood in front of me.

Run while you can, little Larkspur. And while you hide from me, I will   destroy your world.

Acknowledgments

This one's for my dad.

Authors Note

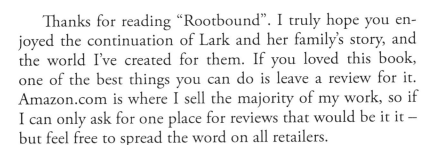

Thanks for reading "Rootbound". I truly hope you enjoyed the continuation of Lark and her family's story, and the world I've created for them. If you loved this book, one of the best things you can do is leave a review for it. Amazon.com is where I sell the majority of my work, so if I can only ask for one place for reviews that would be it it – but feel free to spread the word on all retailers.

Again, thank you for coming on this ride with me, I hope we'll take many more together. The rest of The Elemental Series along with my other novels, are available in both ebook and paperback format on all major retailers.

You will find purchase links on my website at:

www.shannonmayer.com

Enjoy!

About the Author

Shannon Mayer lives in the southwestern tip of Canada with her husband, dog, cats, horse, and cows. When not writing she spends her time staring at immense amounts of rain, herding old people (similar to herding cats) and attempting to stay out of trouble. Especially that last is difficult for her.

She is the *USA Today* Bestselling author of the The Rylee Adamson Novels, The Elemental Series, The Nevermore Trilogy, A Celtic Legacy series and several contemporary romances. Please visit her website for more information on her novels.

www.shannonmayer.com

Ms. Mayer's books can be found at these retailers:

Amazon   iTunes
Barnes & Noble   Smashwords
Kobo

Made in the USA
Charleston, SC
19 July 2016